Dead Men Talk

By Johnny Barnes

May 17, 2020

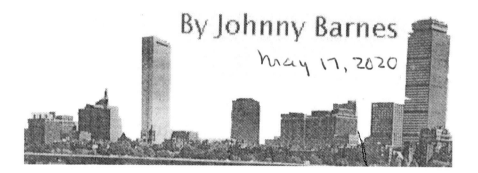

ISBN: 1-4107-0792-X (e-book)
ISBN: 1-4107-0793-8 (Paperback)

This book is printed on acid free paper.

1stBooks – rev. 01/10/03

CHAPTERS

1. SOMETHING BIG 1

2. UNDER THE GUN 8

3. RAIL CAR TO NOWHERE 13

4. THE PACKAGE 17

5. DEEPER, HARDER, FASTER 23

6. SLOW MOTION 29

7. THE NAKED I 39

8. THE DREAM 55

9. THE BOOK 58

10. THE BEAN COUNTER 63

11. WE HAVE NOTHING TO FEAR 71

12. SUSPECTED SERIAL KILLER 77

13. GOOD DREAMS 85

14. BAD DREAMS 87

15. A ROOM WITH A VIEW 89

16. SCOTCH AND REEFER 100

17. RED ARMY ANTS 111

18. HEAVY RAIN 115

19. DEAD RIGHT 130

20. ZEN DETECTIVE IN THE COMBAT ZONE 134

21. THE FIRST TIME I MET THE BLUES 141

22. THE SISTER 145

23. THE TRANSVESTITE & THE HACKER 149

24. AT THE RAT 158

25. THE REGULAR ROTATING SUPER SECRET MONDAY NIGHT POKER GAME 164

26. THE MOVING SURVEILLANCE 170

27. SHAKE, RATTLE, AND ROLL 181

28. THE MEXICAN STANDOFF 192

29. THE RIGHT THING TO DO 199

30. DEAD BODIES 204

31. THE LAST NIGHTMARE 208

32. OFF AT CODE H 213

33. THE LIGHT 217

34. DEAD SERIOUS 232

35. THE TUBE 235

36. BACK FROM THE DEAD 241

37. THE SNAPPER 243

38. UNDER THE STARS 250

39. THE MONSTER LIVES 254

40. DEAD END 264

41. THE MAN WHO WOULD BE KING 274

CHAPTER 1

Something Big

There was a knock on the office door. I jumped up and tried to make it look as if I were busy. Was it opportunity knocking? There was no second chance to make a first impression. I scattered some papers on the desk and took the phone off the hook. I let her in, picked up the phone, and tried to sound important.

"Look, Archer, I'll call you back, but don't move in until I give the word," I said and hung up the phone.

It was then I took stock of the woman before me. Wow, what a package. The signal went up: DANGER—LEGS CROSSING. She had the kind of body that if she walked by a priest, he'd want to turn and check her out.

1

She was about five foot six, built like a centerfold, with long legs, a thin waist, and a set of headlights like an '88 Olds. Her short, jet-black hair was cut straight across above her eyes. Full, red lips, and big, bright, cobalt blue eyes. The lady wore a black silk and lace dress, and an old-fashioned mink stole. She dressed like money. She reeked of money. Big money. Big, old, filthy-rich money.

"I hear you're good," she said.

I wondered if she'd been talking to an old girlfriend or a client.

I waited for her to go on, thinking she already had a high opinion of me, and I didn't want to spoil it by opening my mouth. She came closer. Real close...and looked up into my eyes. "I heard you can help a girl in trouble," she whispered. She smelled good, like a flower garden on a warm summer day. Her deep blue eyes looked right through me, unafraid.

"Well..." I managed to stammer, "I don't know if I can take another case," I said, giving her the standard line.

She moved closer. It seemed to get warmer. Maybe it was the night air. We embraced. I got a warm feeling down below...and it got a lot warmer when she shoved a roll of $100 bills in my pants pocket. Deep in my pants pocket. As I looked into her eyes, she kissed me passionately.

Suddenly, the outer office doors opened, and I could hear feet shuffling and people entering. Then the inner office door burst open, and there, blocking all light from the doorway, stood the largest, fattest human being I had ever seen.

In a guttural voice that sounded like it oozed from a sewer, the fat man growled, "Get in the car, Baby!"

"No! This can't go on!" My new client cried.

Now, I'm not a big man—I'm about five-ten and one hundred sixty-five pounds soaking wet, but the man who stood before me had to be closer to seven feet than six. He must have weighed an incredible six hundred and fifty pounds or more. He had black, greasy hair stretched across his scalp and huge cheeks of blubber. He was absolutely grotesque. The buttons of his shirt appeared ready to burst open from the rolls of fat. He had an ass that stuck out like the caboose on a freight train. His huge dark suit barely covered the girth of his belly as he squeezed through the door. I could smell the strong musty scent of his cologne. His fingernails were manicured, slightly rose-colored, and glossy. He had legs with thighs as thick as tree trunks, thinning calves, skinny ankles, and little bird feet covered by loafers with tassels on them.

I don't like people yelling in my office. It's not polite. Before this domestic brawl went any further, since it was my office, and in an effort to keep the situation from escalating, I proposed reason be our guiding light and we all separate and discuss this in the morning.

"You shut up right now, Flatfoot, or you'll be smilin' without teeth!" was the response, with a voice so husky it could pull a dog sled.

As if on cue, a four-foot-small, well-dressed, dark skinned man slid in from behind the larger, holding what appeared to be a .45 caliber semi-automatic, (much too large a heater for a dwarf, but it does make a large hole). He too, had his black hair slicked down, combed across his head, and wore a similar dark suit, just like the much larger version.

I was beginning to feel the value of the roll of $100 bills in my pocket was diminishing rapidly.

My client, whose name I didn't yet know, was fumbling in her purse, possibly for a handkerchief. She instead produced a small caliber handgun of her own, which slipped from her purse along with some keys and clanked across to the center of the floor. The midget stepped forward to retrieve this weapon, but things had gone far enough. With one motion I kicked the gun from his hand, caught the semi-automatic, and pointed it at the small man's head.

"It looks like I'll be asking the questions now. Maybe we'll order some Chinese food and have a group therapy session."

The Fat Man just sort of grunted, but the midget seemed to tense up. He was going to go for me, even though I was pointing a gun at his head. I could no longer contain myself and let go with a stream of expletives, which I will leave here deleted. I was now the ringmaster for this sideshow.

"Tell the squirt to calm down real fast, Fat Boy, or we'll need two ambulances! Or at least one and a half." I added.

I was calling the shots, and I was considering making them head shots. But I didn't know what was going on. I didn't know any of these people. Was the circus in town?

The midget obeyed his master's command to sit. I didn't have a chair big enough for The Large One. He sat in the middle of the couch and it creaked under the strain.

I had the floor.

"You all seem to know who I am, and since you're such good friends, why don't we introduce ourselves. You can tell me why you're here, while I wonder why I'm not calling the police yet."

I motioned to Fat Boy to start. I was already feeling guilty about calling him Fat Boy. I'm usually a sensitive guy.

"My name is Thaddeus Reno, I'm an eco-management executive and—"

"He takes garbage to the dump, Jack!" What's-her-name shouted.

"Waste management and recycling is big business and quite profitable," he growled. This guy must have something stuck in his throat. Then Big Boy offered, "There's always a need for lots of security, you know."

He must have seen I was slightly offended. "Management of course, er...uh..." he added.

6

What's this guy think, I'm a security guard? I have standards…They're low, but I have standards. Sure, I've done plenty of low-level work. I've served subpoenas and repossessed cars. I've done security guard work, when I was young, and still on occasion. It fills in the holes in my schedule. Yeah, I'm just a working stiff, and maybe Reno thought of me as a flatfoot, a snoop, a dick, gumshoe, or a peep, but I'm a detective!

Mr. Big continued. "I don't want to waste your time sir, this is just a domestic situation, a lovers' quarrel, if you will sir…We'll all just find our way out then, and, eh—Come on, Baby! We're so sorry about this little mix-up."

The midget was helping Mr. King Size up, while "Baby," maybe that was her name, shrieked.

"I won't go with you, Reno! You'll never get the book!" she screamed.

That's when I made the mistake. As I turned away for one second to look at "Baby," I saw a glimmer and felt the thud of a blunt object against my thick skull and the lights went out.

CHAPTER 2

Under the Gun

At first, I thought I was waking up to the worst hangover I'd ever had. Then I wished it were the worst hangover I'd ever had. I wasn't sure where I was or who I was. It took an effort to get slowly up onto my chair. I was still seeing stars. I put my hands to my head and felt around. No blood, but what a bump, halfway between my left eye and my hairline. A goose egg.

I didn't have any ice in the office, so I put a cold metal spoon on the bump and had a couple of medicinal shots of scotch. I washed up and checked the damage in the mirror. I tried to pull a shock of my red hair over the bump but it didn't cover it.

Maybe I should call the cops. Maybe I should've called earlier. My brothers in blue would love to hear how I was holding some armed thugs at gun point, but decided not to call the cops, and while conducting my own investigation ended up getting knocked out by a midget. I would hear about it for the next twenty years.

"Hey, Jack Kelly's workin' the case—maybe he'll get knocked out by a midget!" I could hear them laughing.

I've worked big cases; homicides, shootings, abductions, robberies, burglary rings, gang wars. Crime was my business, and business was good. I've solved important crimes, maybe saved a life here and there. But what would I be remembered for? What would I hear? "Hey, Jack! I heard you got knocked out by a midget." I sighed and shook my throbbing head.

It was a hot and steamy night, late in the Indian Summer in Boston. I walked over to the office windows and opened them the rest of the way, looking down on the streets of Chinatown four floors below.

Did I have a client? What was her name? What was the case? The money was still in my pocket. I supposed that meant I'd be

9

hearing from her again, if just to get back the roll of hundreds she'd stuffed down my pants.

Still, I didn't like it. You couldn't barge into my office, waving a gun around and pistol whip this detective. Well, maybe just that once. But information was my game and investigation was my claim to fame. My thing. My turf. And I wanted to know my enemy. But no farmer ever plowed a field by turning it over in his mind. It was time to get my hands dirty. It was time to get on the case. Mr. Big Boy was in my world now.

Chubby was the main man and the only name I had. Thaddeus Reno, if that really was his name. Eco-waste management-executive—garbage man. I'd start with the Department of Motor Vehicles. The DMV would give me his full name, address, date of birth, vehicle plate numbers and more. It was a good place to start, and all a good private investigator needed to start a file on someone. In a week I'd know what property he owned, where it was and how much it was worth.

I could obtain credit card information as detailed as what size shirt he bought, at exactly what time he bought it, and where. How much gas he put in his car, and where he was when it was put in. Intimate details like what he ate for lunch, how much it cost him and where and when he ate it.

If he has a partner, I'd check the Bureau of Corporations and eventually find out who it was. Spouse information, family names, and residences. With a limited surveillance I would have photos of the subject and his associates. I could learn his political affinity at Voter Registration, and start to chart his family tree if needed.

And that's public information. If I picked up and went through his garbage—which is considered abandoned property—I could get all kinds of info as detailed as the brand of cereal he eats. Bank account numbers and money figures, phone bill information and whom he calls. A talk with a couple of Fat Boy's acquaintances and the picture will start filling in like a Polaroid snapshot.

Surveillance can dig deep into the private world of a person. Very intimate moments can be seen and recorded with powerful lenses. Voices can be heard with powerful or strategically placed microphones. The more I prepare, the luckier I'll get. In an investigation, as in golf, it's the follow through that makes the difference.

Yes, the Big Man was in my world now!

But I still didn't know who the beautiful woman with the ice blue eyes and jet-black hair was. I could storm out of the detective agency like the Blue Knight to rescue her, but I wouldn't know which way to storm. That would have to wait. I had a plan, but it was 3:15 a.m. and after another shot of scotch, I was going to put this patient to bed. I strapped on my shoulder holster and got my .45 caliber Colt Combat Commander out of the wall safe.

Oh, man's inhumanity to man.

CHAPTER 3

Rail Car To Nowhere

At 7:45 a.m. that morning, I got a call from Sergeant Bill Rogers of the Homicide Unit of the Boston Police Department. He wanted me to come down to the abandoned trains on Atlantic Avenue near Pier 4 by Anthony's restaurant. He said he'd send a car, and I knew this was more than a social visit. I told him I'd drive myself down. I ran myself through a shower like a '57 Cadillac going through a Main Street car wash. One cup of coffee getting dressed and one for the ride to Pier 4.

The sun was burning through the early morning fog as I pulled up to the open fields on the waterfront next to Pier 4. The deserted fields were the graveyard stop for some of Boston's rail cars, but the area looked more like abandoned property. There were five squad cars, two unmarked cars, and the mobile crime lab van parked around the perimeter of what appeared to be a crime scene. There was more activity by plain-clothes units around the second car in, of four abandoned rail cars. I was wondering why Sergeant Rogers wanted me there, when he and Sergeant Jim Watson stepped out of the rail car.

"Jack, you know Sergeant Rogers from Homicide. He wants to ask you a few questions about Bella Pavoni," Jim Watson said, twirling his long, thick handlebar mustache.

Well, I was as much in the dark as ever. I was getting tired of knowing less about what was going on than everybody else.

I guess from my blank face, it was apparent to these two men who read faces for a living I didn't know what was going on. Sergeant Rogers motioned me to the rail car doorway. As we stepped into the musty, old abandoned rail car, forensic technicians were taping paper bags onto the hands of a corpse. Flashbulbs were snapping. Before me, I saw the woman who had come to me for help lying on the damp, dirty rail car floor. Her neck was twisted hideously around. Her eyes were staring straight ahead—staring at me.

The hair stood up on the back of my neck. The oxygen had been sucked out of the air, and the smell of death had taken its place. I felt like I had just been hit in the head again. The lights seemed to grow dim, and I wanted to run out of the rail car.

"Let's go outside," I mumbled quickly.

As we stepped out of the rail car, I took a deep breath of the morning sea air, and tried to focus.

Sergeant Rogers handed me one of my business cards. "We think this may be the serial killer's work, Jack. She had a business card with your name and number on it, in her pocket. We'd like to know why."

I didn't know how much to tell them—I didn't know much. After all, I had discovered my client's name posthumously. Bill Rogers and I had worked together before, when I was still a city detective, and I knew if I gave him a little, he'd give me a little.

"Bill, I didn't even know her name."

I told the detective of my nocturnal visit by the traveling sideshow that had passed through my office the previous night. I padded the story a little, leaving out the kiss, the cash, the guns, and getting whacked in the head by the midget. By now the lump on my head was reduced to a red and purple smudge under a shock of red hair. As improbable and ridiculous a story as I told, he seemed to buy it. I thought I detected a look from him that indicated he thought this poor private detective didn't have a clue.

Bill told me I'd have to come in to the Detective Division and write out a formal statement later in the day. He made it sound routine, but I was beginning to realize I might have been, at least to his knowledge, the last to see Bella Pavoni alive.

I needed time to think, and they were going to be processing the crime scene for hours, so I told Rogers I'd be in the station by noon. It wasn't like I was a suspect…

CHAPTER 4

The Package

When I left the Detective Division at Boston Police Headquarters on Berkeley Street in the late afternoon, I didn't know much more than I had when I'd gone in. Sergeant Rogers was backing off the serial killer theory. When I asked whom this Thaddeus Reno was, I got little more than a grumble from Rogers. He did tell me Reno must be connected to someone "upstairs," and he was up to his neck in garbage.

Bella Pavoni, though, was no hooker. From what I could read from Detective Rogers, she was from an old Boston family, a rich and influential family that made their money from cranberries, politics, and real estate. There was pressure from upstairs to tighten the screws and find out how she ended up in a rail car with a broken neck. I couldn't forget the way she stared at me in death, as if she were asking me for help—rescue that never came, a client that was dead before I knew her name.

According to the television and newspapers, it was "SIX FOR KILLER." There had been five other murders involving similar methods, but Bella Pavoni had been the first woman, and the first from a prominent Boston family.

I felt like I was caught up in a wave of events, and the surf was up. In less than twenty-four hours I had been hired, pistol whipped, my client was dead, I was an unlikely suspect in a possible serial killing, and I hadn't had a proper breakfast yet. But since the latter was the one thing I could do something about, I went to the downtown Mug N' Muffin and tried to gain control of my life with some bacon and eggs. I hadn't had much sleep—maybe a couple of cups of coffee would clear the cobwebs from my head.

After my late afternoon breakfast, I put my car back in the downtown garage and walked the few blocks to my little office in Chinatown. The streets were buzzing as the supper hour approached.

The delivery trucks carrying fresh poultry, fish, and vegetables finished their deliveries as the Chinatown restaurants geared up for the evening. I took the elevator up to my fourth-floor office, in a small building wedged between two restaurants.

I decided to sit down with pencil and paper and try to sort out the situation. I wanted to be in charge. I was trained at the Police Academy to take charge. I had been in the dark long enough—it was time I got in the driver's seat. Captain of my ship. Who did these people think I was, anyway? I'm a goddamn detective.

The pad and paper filled up with a few names, a few facts, a time line, a short list of events, but I didn't know a lot. That was something I was going to remedy. Thaddeus Reno. He seemed like a good place to start.

I started making phone calls. The first call was to Sergeant James Watson, who I had seen at Bella Pavoni's crime scene at the rail car earlier that morning. Sergeant Watson wasn't one of the lead investigators on the case, he wasn't even working Homicide anymore. He had probably been asked to come to the scene because he had been a partner of mine when I'd worked Homicide. He had put in his twenty-five years, and even though he was only forty-six years old, he could retire.

Watson was still a Boston cop, although he'd almost lost his shield a few years back. Jim had gotten busted for allegedly urging a prostitute to clean the knobs in his cruiser for free one night. They were parked down by the waterfront, in the cruiser. Jim's pants were down around his ankles when a Boston Herald photographer snapped a picture and took off in a van. It made the morning edition. It was definitely a classic case of the little head doing the thinking for the big head.

Jim Watson went from a hotshot homicide detective to a desk in burglary. But he still had the quick access to information a policeman could get. Like criminal history, logs of police responses to a certain location, aliases, associates, automobiles, and if the subject is a criminal, intelligence gathered by various units such as burglary, the drug unit, vice, and homicide.

James Watson owed me...big time. His sister had twin daughters, by some rat out in Colorado. She and the Colorado rat got married, had the twins, and played house. One day when Watson's sister came home from work, the kids were gone, the furniture gone, and the Colorado rat was gone. She moved back east and rebuilt her shattered life, but the maternal instinct got the better of her. She needed those twin girls. The police out in Colorado weren't much help. With their heavy caseload, this custody dispute just wasn't a high priority. She'd turned to Watson, and he'd turned to me. Watson couldn't pay the kind of hourly rates private detective agencies required, and I couldn't ask him to.

I'd done allot of phone work, and tracked the father and twins through five states. I mentioned to a relative of the Colorado rats that the mother was quite well off now, (so I embellished...all right I lied,) and offered an unspecified reward. I got a phone call in three days, and within two more, I'd located the twins. Mother flew the twins home for a small remuneration to the father. The nieces now live, happily ever after, just two blocks from Uncle James Watson. It was one of the rare and elusive happy endings seldom occurring in detective work. Yes, James Watson owed me.

I gave him the names Thaddeus Reno and Bella Pavoni, and a bare bones sketch of what was going on, most of which he already knew, and he said he'd get back to me in the morning.

I put my head down on the desk and began to ponder the prospect that if my client were dead, there would be no further payments. I felt a certain obligation to Bella Pavoni. She'd paid in advance. But it was a police matter now. Yet it was still a matter I was involved in, even if not by choice.

The phone rang. The muffled male voice said, "The package is for you." And he hung up.

Just when did I lose control? Who the hell was that? Must've been a wrong number. I decided to head for my girlfriend's house, to get some sleep…or whatever else I could. I stubbed out the last of my Jamaican cigar, took a last shot of scotch, turned out the lights, and walked out the office door. Then I tripped over the box.

It didn't move. Whatever was in there, it was heavy. It was about three feet square, made from heavy cardboard, and taped closed. It didn't have any address or writing on it. Since it was in front of my office door, I thought maybe I would open it. I should have left it.

Inside the package was one midget…quite dead.

CHAPTER 5

Deeper, Harder, Faster

Sergeant Rogers was not happy about being called to the crime scene of another apparent murder victim, but he wasn't going to get any sympathy from me. Dead bodies were getting on my nerves, too. Why me? I wasn't listed first in the yellow pages under detective agencies—Alpha Security was. Why weren't they getting this business? I sure as hell didn't need it. I hadn't had a good night's sleep and the homicide squad was spending more time with me than with their wives.

But still, I had a distinct feeling that for the first time since Bella Pavoni walked into my office, I had a clearer sense of the events taking place around me. I had a creeping feeling someone was setting

23

me up. Someone was spending far too much time involving me. Why me? Sure I'd called that guy "Fat Boy," but why the package? The midget whacked me, so what? Was this a gift? Was this meant to appease me? I would have settled for flowers, or an apology.

The BPD and state forensics investigators checked the package while uniformed cops strung yellow crime scene tape and blocked off the hallway with a sheet. They all stepped aside when the medical examiner arrived. The M.E. examined, and the lab boys photographed every step as they unfolded the naked midget. The body kept folding back up into the fetal position, rigor mortis having set in. After the deceased had been stretched out, let go, and had sprung back into a ball three or four times, the M.E. instructed the assisting officers to stretch him out and hold him that way while he examined the body for a preliminary diagnosis of the cause of death. Even though the corpse had dark skin, bruising around the neck was evident. A bone protruded just under the skin on the back of his neck. The M.E. made a small, bloodless incision over the left hip and jammed a thermometer up into the liver in an attempt to determine the time of death. He probed the body in every available nook and cranny. He lifted, twisted, and bent the limbs, checking the stage of rigor mortis that worked its way from the head.

I thought about the small dead man. He had been a person. He had a life, before it was snuffed out. He was someone who had a soul, a spirit. Someone who was manipulated in this mystery, as I had been.

After a quick ten-minute examination, the M.E., Dr. Frank Ryan, walked from the hall into my office, where Bill Rogers and I sat.

"What's the prelim, Doc?" Sergeant Rogers asked.

The doctor looked back at the corpse, slowly shaking his head. He took off the dirty rubber examination gloves he had just used to probe the dead midget and dropped them in my wastebasket. Thanks Doc.

"Did he tell you who killed him, Doc?" I asked.

"He'll tell me the cause of death. He'll tell me about his last meal and what time he ate it. If he drank alcohol or took drugs. The time of his death. You know detective," he told me raising one eyebrow, "dead men talk.

"There is some Rigor Mortis in the upper torso, the cornea is clouding, postmortem lividity indicates he was placed in the box shortly after death. I'll have to check the stomach contents to close in on the exact time of death…"

The doctor went on as if he were addressing a class at Harvard Medical School. "The spinal column, a clavicle compression, the anterior longitudinal ligament—not a severing, the inter-clavicular fractures of the Dontoid process, in the neural arch between the cervical vertebrae along the—"

"Come on, Doc! In English, please. I didn't graduate from med. school since I saw you last time," Rogers pleaded.

"Broken neck," The doctor stated, drifting back towards the corpse, once again the object of his attention, if not affection.

Sergeant Rogers hadn't asked me any direct questions. I think he was hoping I'd open up and tell all I knew, except I was even more in the dark than ever. The dwarf had no clothes, no jewelry, and no identification.

"Jack," Sergeant Rogers said at last. "Now, I've got more than a half a dozen homicides, and the last two are linked to you. Bella

Pavoni's family and some other bigwigs are all over upstairs, and I need some answers."

After a long pause, I said, "Bill, you still got that boat?"

"Yeah, put it back in the water every April."

"You still go down around Martha's Vineyard and the Islands for the bluefish?"

"Jack, you know I go every chance I get. My wife says she's gonna leave me if I don't stop goin' fishin' every chance…Gee I'm gonna miss her!" Bill loved the old jokes. "I'm hoping we can go together sometime. I know some great spots, and I've got a Fish Finder now." He added.

"Bill, I don't know why I got this package. I don't know this dead midget. Bella Pavoni, the midget, and the Fat Man came to my office. They didn't tell me why. I can only guess Bella wanted protection from Fatboy, and the police don't normally provide extended bodyguard service. Maybe Mr. Big was actually afraid of me, afraid I would start looking into his business affairs. I'm guessing. I don't know anything else. That's what scares me."

27

Rogers was looking at me, weighing and digesting, adding and subtracting, analyzing the data. After all, he was a big city detective, and that's why he got the big bucks.

I reversed roles. I looked Rogers straight in the eye.

"Bill, what can you tell me? Look, I'm in the middle of something I don't have a handle on. I could help you put two and two together. I'm tired of being played like a pinball machine. I've got some motivation here—I don't like the fact there's dead bodies around and you're lookin' at me! Information is what I need!"

He mumbled something about an official investigation in my direction. I thought I'd been talking one-on-one, man-to-man, brother to brother. Jesus, Bill was playing it close to the vest. I guess I was in deeper than I thought. Maybe the pressure from the top was heavier than I thought.

At first it seemed like this run-around was out of line, I was being treated like a civilian. Or worse. Maybe I was being treated like a suspect.

CHAPTER 6

Slow Motion

It was 1 a.m. and I still hadn't had a good night's sleep. I don't function well after a prolonged period of sleep depravation, accompanied by poor diet. Even though the adrenaline of being in a threatening situation had carried me, I knew I had to recharge my batteries. And even though Sergeant Rogers had spared me the "Don't leave town" speech, I knew I couldn't take off for parts unknown. I knew I had to get some release—I knew what I had to do.

The elements…light, dark, snow, wind, rain…you can't control them…but you can use them to your advantage. I decided to slip in, under the cover of darkness.

I turned off my headlights and coasted to a stop in the quiet residential neighborhood near Harvard Square. As I slipped out of my car, I realized how black a night it was. It was perfect. There was no moon in the night sky, no streetlights shining nearby. It seemed as if everyone in the neighborhood was asleep. I ducked off from the sidewalk and crawled through the front yard along the bushes. A dog barked down the block. I waited. As I moved from behind the bushes to the front porch stairs, I saw the street was empty.

The front door was unlocked and opened without a creak. I was inside.

There wasn't a sound in the house. I moved through the hallway and up the stairs slowly, hardly making a sound. I moved very slowly, even the slight creaking of the floorboards seemed natural. I knew which bedroom she was in, and the bedroom door was partly open. I moved through the door and across the floor silently, moving ever so slowly and slipped onto her bed. I knew what I had to do.

I cupped one hand over her mouth and put the other in between her legs. She was startled and made some muffled sounds, but I was in charge. Her green eyes widened as she arose from her slumber to see me hovering over her. She resisted at first, and then less and less as she realized I held her in my control. She moaned and struggled against me. She was warm. I moved my hand and kissed her open mouth deeply, pinning her against the bed as she tried to bite my lip. I pulled my head back, then quickly moved back in, kissing her hot lips again.

She moaned some more, still struggling, and then went limp. Then she put her arms around me and kissed me hungrily.

"You're late tonight, bad boy," she said coyly.

"Would you hold my gun?" I asked as I undressed.

"Is it a big gun?"

"It's not that big, but it does the job."

"If I touch it, will it go off?"

"Don't rub the lamp if you don't want the genie to come out."

She giggled as I pressed on.

"Did you know that the average sexual encounter lasts about fifteen minutes?" I asked her.

"No."

"Well I don't mean to brag, but...I think I could cut that time in half."

She laughed. And then we made long, slow, love.

Sleep. Long sleep. Long, slow sleep. I needed it so badly. I'll try to dream about the nightclub I've always wanted to open some day. "Johnny's Jazz and Blues Club."

Maybe some answers would come to me in my sleep. Maybe it was like Confucius said: "Man who go to sleep with problem, wake up with solution in hand." But that would be too easy.

My girlfriend says, "A hard man is good to find."

Things always come the hard way with me, and tonight was no exception.

It started the same way it always did. The same feeling, like some one walking over my grave. The same nightmare. Some of the details were interchangeable, but the elements were always the same.

The Chase. I could hardly run—my legs felt like they were stuck in mud or quicksand. I'm trying to run through the woods. Time seems to move in slow motion, and slows to a stop. I could hear myself breathing, and it became so quiet I thought I could hear the wings of flying insects. It's dark, and something was moving closer to me, something I couldn't see. But it saw me. I struggled. It likes me to struggle. Its' senses were sharper. Its' sense of smell and hearing were more acute, more sensitive. It could sense heat, and read thermals. It began to relentlessly track me down.

It was inevitable, unavoidable, and inescapable. It homed in on me. No matter where I tried to hide, no matter what corners I took, it kept coming. I knew I had to move faster, run harder. I had to get away…I was in Its' world now.

I shot bolt upright in a cold sweat.

The next morning I took a long, hot shower and had a hot breakfast. I got to my little office in Chinatown by 9:15, and wasn't greeted by any surprise packages. The newspapers hadn't had time to get out a story on the dead midget, but news radio was pumping it as the lead story. At least they weren't linking the midget's death to the supposed serial killer…yet.

I called Sergeant Jim Watson. Jim had heard about my "package" at briefing that morning. He told me he had heard the homicide unit was under a lot of pressure to bring somebody in. I got a chill when my old partner mumbled something about this being a major, official investigation now. Man, this guy owed me and I had to remind him.

"Jim, how are your twin nieces doing? You still coaching the twins' softball team?"

"Okay, Jack, I get your drift. I've got part of the file here, somewhere. It's going up to Homicide. Ah, here it is. The midget's name was Benny Lopes, a Portuguese man from New Bedford. He used to collect money for the Irish, Italian, and Portuguese bookies there, running numbers from bar to bar. He was, pardon the expression, a small-time operator with the fishermen's union, too. When Thaddeus Reno's waste management company wanted the contracts in the New Bedford area, Benny Lopes lined up all the small-time crime families, the restaurants and fish houses. Everybody else fell in line eventually. Then he graduated to Reno's traveling sideshow."

I listened carefully, but said nothing.

"Thaddeus Reno is quite a piece of work," he continued.

"He grew up in South Boston, raised by his Irish mother. She suffered from, it says here, hyperostesis frontalis interna, a hormonal disorder which made her very, very, fat, and hairy. Honest to God that's what it says here. His father was Italian, a musician, traveling with a big band from New York City. After little Thaddeus was born, his father kept on traveling, never to return.

"Reno has no criminal record, not even as a juvenile. Word is, he was a mama's boy who became a flunky and did odd jobs for the Irish mob. He was a bouncer at some of the Mob bars in Southie, until some of the wise guys put their money behind his garbage management business. Then he went from driving one of five garbage trucks to owning and operating a fleet of shiny brand new disposal vehicles. You know Boston politics. A citywide contract, then countywide and state- wide contracts, and in the span of a few years he became a very rich man. He hooked up with the Boston families, and was contributing to political campaigns, like the Lieutenant Governor's. And he's a regular patron of the arts. That's how he met Bella Pavoni.

"Jack, you ought to be careful, there's a lot of pressure from upstairs. This guy Reno, he's so crooked he needs a corkscrew to get his pants on. There's a serial killer out there. We're coming up on an election year, and the talk is the Lieutenant Governor is about to be reported as engaging in sexual misconduct and some kind of economic improprieties."

"Sounds like he doesn't know if he's a Democrat or a Republican," I stated wryly, but Watson didn't laugh.

"Jack, somebody's gonna get sent over for this soon, and I don't want you to be in the ejection seat. They'll hang you out to dry."

I thought about what Sergeant Watson said. Coming from him, it was a cold slap of reality. If I didn't take this seriously, I could wind up in jail. Up the river, in the slammer, in stir, the cooler, the can, the big house, the hoosegow, the joint, the jug. Prison. The state's restructuring, redevelopment, and rehabilitation center...Hotel Hell.

A case is a case, but I was beginning to realize I was the client. I wished I could give back the roll of thirty- six $100 bills Bella Pavoni shoved down my pants. Watson told me he would check some more, but officially, he was not communicating any case information to me. I got his drift.

As soon as I got off the phone, it rang again. And again. Two Boston newspapers and three television stations all wanted to know about "the package." I told them I couldn't comment on an ongoing investigation. Christ, I sounded like I was still a city cop—only this was a little closer to home. Maybe I should get a lawyer. Maybe I should read myself my rights. I had the right to remain silent. Anything I said may be held against me and used in a court of law. I have the right to an attorney…

So I called my brother, a practicing attorney down on Cape Cod, and told him everything that had happened, just in case.

I felt I was being sucked into a black hole.

It was very late when I got back to my girlfriend's apartment in Harvard Square and crawled into bed. I needed some affection. Or maybe I just needed to do it. The Old Mating Dance. The Horizontal Boogie. The Wild Thing.

Maybe I could wake the little woman. Her long straight auburn hair flowed down against her naked back to her waist. Her bright green eyes were shut tight, and her breathing was deep and regular. She had been horseback riding that day at my father's stables, and was sleeping like a farm hand. Girls and women seem to love horses and horseback riding. Maybe it's the rocking motion. Or the trotting. Or when that beast breaks into a canter. There's a heavy rhythm thing working there. The four hooves are hitting the ground in a syncopated beat, the horse's breathing is heavy, hot, and lathered. Maybe it's the power thing. She realizes she's on top and in control of fifteen hundred pounds of wild beast between her legs. Maybe that's it.

I tried to gently wake her up, but it was no good. She didn't respond. Women need to be wined and dined. Flirted with, pursued, cajoled, and petted. They need a certain amount of foreplay...

All I needed was to hear "Come and get it!"

CHAPTER 7

The Naked i

The next morning, it was time to hit the streets. Even when I was a beat cop, knowing what was happening always paid off. I had to start working my sources, develop new contacts. After all, I'm a detective.

I drove around, shooting the breeze with prostitutes, street people (urban campers for the politically correct,) bookies, drug dealers, security guards, movers and shakers of the underworld. I tried to look at things without the anxiety and frustration that came with being under the gun. I had a deceased Bella Pavoni, a bankroll of $3600, the Garbage Man, something about "the book," a dead midget, and a serial killer.

When Bella Pavoni came to me, she'd wanted protection. This was no ordinary domestic situation. The Fat Man wanted more than just his woman back. He wanted "the book." And Bella had it. If it was the Blimp who killed Bella later on that night, maybe he didn't get his "book" back. The brutal marks on her neck and the cold intense stare I saw on Bella Pavoni's face told me she'd gone down fighting.

By six o'clock I had learned from my street sources that the Large One was staying at a lush condo in Chelsea, on Admirals Hill, an upscale development of town houses overlooking the Boston Harbor and Bunker Hill, the shipping lanes, and the Chelsea end of the Mystic Tobin Bridge. He sometimes stayed on his sixty-foot luxury tugboat by the Charlestown Navy Yard. He had his sticky fingers into drugs, prostitution, and had a small gang of dementoids that did everything from strong-arm collection to art museum burglaries and armored car hold-ups. The midget had been his right hand man for the last three years, I was told.

It was early in the evening. I wandered through Chinatown into the Combat Zone; the section of Boston reserved for First

Amendment bookstores, adult movie theaters, and adult clubs. The inhabitants there were not the same type of shoppers you'd see in the rest of the downtown area. There were drunks, junkies, pimps, druggies, street hustlers, bums fighting over a bottle of cheap wine, hookers working the streets. There were strip joints with names like The Pussy Cat Lounge, The Glass Slipper, The Intermission Lounge, Good Time Charlie's, and The Naked i, which boasted an "ALL NUDE COLLEGE GIRL REVUE."

I went into the 2 O'clock Lounge for a beer. It's an elegantly sleazy Boston strip club, a classic. There was a long horseshoe bar with a runway type stage down the middle, running the length of the club. All of the walls were painted flat black, and only the stage was brightly lit. There were booths stretching down along one wall into a dark corner.

After the dancers left the stage, they were expected to work the crowd. Customers would buy the dancers champagne for twenty-five dollars and sit in the dark booths and try to get a little more for their money.

The strippers offered me a moment's distraction from the case. Bouncing mounds of round, tight, firm flesh. Faces made up with eye shadow, and red lipstick. All hair and high heels, moving suggestively. They mostly had class acts at the 2 O'clock. Nothing like "Mary and the Disappearing Vegetables" although there was one "exotic" dancer who looked like she had just pulled a double shift at the Mustang Ranch.

Then I stopped by the Naked i and I got a shot of scotch and a beer, on the house from my longtime pal Ed McGee, who had been the bartender there for the last twelve years. Ed was from the old school. To him, it didn't matter what you did, as long as you did it well. He was an ex-marine, and had been a quarterback in high school. He was tall, rugged, and confident, and if you didn't mind hearing over and over about the championship game, in which he threw for three touchdowns and ran for one more, then you'd like Ed.

Ed and I go way back. Once upon a time I'd played guitar in a blues band and Ed was my tour manager and soundman. We made records, traveled, got radio airplay, did television shows, the whole thing. We'd been through a lot together. He knew me well.

42

He knew all about the serial killer, the midget, and the Big Man. This guy knew more than the new computer at police headquarters. And Ed had perspective. He made me feel that some one else knew what was going on. Maybe I'm not totally alone in a dark and foreboding void, a maze that leads nowhere. A tiny powerless speck of cosmic dust, amounting to nothing. Is the earth off its axis? Is it spinning uncontrollably into the void? Nah.

But if the only moral and spiritual support I could get was from a bartender at a strip joint in the Combat Zone, then I was in trouble.

"Your pal Bob was in here asking for you last night," he said.

"Who? Bob? What's he look like?"

"Heavyset, looks like a weight lifter. Unshaven, with those little potholes in his face. Pock marks. Short blonde hair. Military cut. Talks with a bit of a lisp? He tells a great story about you and him trackin' that murderer fugitive to Texas when you were cops, only to find him dead in a motel room."

"That sounds like fun, Ed, but I've never been to Texas."

The look on Ed's face told me we both realized he'd been had. Somebody was still interested in me, but it didn't sound like the cops. My mind began to race again.

"Don't look at me, take it up with him." Ed nodded to the rear of the bar, where the individual previously described stood, staring at me. I didn't know him, and a sinking feeling told me I didn't want to.

The guy fit right in, with a cheap, shiny, dark red suit, and a cigarette dangling from his lip. He could have been a bouncer, or a pimp, or a loan shark, or a john out for a good time. He could be a guy out on a work release program from Walpole State Prison, or as they call it now, in this kinder, gentler time, Cedar Junction.

Some guys have a look that can kill, or freeze you in your tracks. Some look like they're tough, and some are. They command respect. And there are some guys that look tough and have a menacing presence, but return their cold stare and give them a couple of slaps, and they turn into whimpering jellyfish. I wondered which kind he was.

I wanted to see if he was after me. I walked slowly into the back bar. He didn't follow. I walked out the back door, walked around to the front, and entered again. He had turned and was facing the entrance, looking straight at me. I got a chill. He looked like a professional.

I sat back down in the same spot at the bar. Ed gave me another round. He had one of the girls bring the stranger, or "Bob," as he had called himself the night before, a Captain Morgan rum and Coke, the same drink he had ordered the night before. I felt like a moth being drawn to a flame, but I had to play this out. Bob came over and took the stool to my left.

"Bob! I haven't seen you since, what was it, Texas?"

The man didn't smile or flinch. He took a long drink off his rum and coke. He looked at me very coldly and business like and said, real low, "You got something that don't belong to you. Give it up or your world is going to come crashing down around you!"

"That's no way to say hello, Bob."

I guess I've got a habit of joking around too much, 'cause I could see his jaw tighten whenever I called him "Bob".

45

"Bob, Robert, come on now, why so stern? Bob, Bobby, haven't seen you since Mexico, or was it Texas? Billy-Bob, Bob, Bobby, Bob Baby. Robby Boy. My boy Bob."

He was ready to rip me up. His eyes were widening, his jaw muscles were tightening, his teeth were clenching, and his eyes began to blink.

"Bob, long time no see. Where you livin' now?"

He seemed to be debating whether to whack me right there.

We looked at each other. I don't know if it was the scotch or the fact I was tired of being used as a pinball in this game, but I said, "So how's little Bob?"

"Look, we can do business," he said trying to collect himself. "You won't get hurt and I'll be outta here faster than a white man through Harlem. You give me the item that don't belong to you, and that's that. You don't get hurt and I don't have to hurt you. Everybody's happy, capisce?"

I might have responded to him, as one professional to another, but when he pronounced "Capeesh," I felt like I was in some cheap B movie, with the role of Bob being played by a tacky, cut-rate heavy with the finesse of a bulldozer.

"Capeesh?" Could he be referring to the Italian word "Capisce", meaning to understand?

"Well Bob...Bobby. Since this is our first date and since I got what you want, don't you think you ought to send me flowers or bring me some candy, offer me dinner, or say something sweet, Bob? Tickle me a little. You know, play with me a little bit, or blow in my ear. You know Bobby Boy, warm me up a little before you try to bang me. Okay Bobby Baby?"

It was all he could take. He began to stare at me, wide- eyed and tense. He began to reach inside his jacket, but I had my hand on my .45 and stuck it right down between his legs. We didn't move. Our eyes were locked. With my left hand, I reached across and lifted the shot of scotch to my lips and drained it. I talked to him slowly and deliberately as I stared unblinking into his eyes.

"You tell the Garbage Man I want out. You tell him to stay away. I don't want to play anymore. And I don't want to see you anymore,

Bob. I'm breaking up with you. We're through. It's over." I pulled the .45 back under my coat but kept it pointing at his midsection.

Bob cleared off the bar with one sweep of his arm. Every glass and bottle went crashing in every direction. The whole place came to a standstill. There was dead silence, except for the jukebox playing "Rip It Up" by Little Richard.

Bob stood up, turned, and walked out the door.

I don't like pulling a gun. It can get you in deep trouble, fast. But I don't like someone else calling the shots in my life. Not some depraved steroid punk, or the Fat Man who's pulling his strings. I can screw things up for myself, I didn't need these guys.

I had some marinated beef tips and Lazy Man's lobster at a booth in the back lounge. The Celtics-Bulls game was on television but even though I looked up at it often, I was somewhere else. I called the answering machine at the office from the pay phone and lit a cigar. I was glad I had a solid meal under my belt, even though the phrase "the Last Supper" kept coming to mind. "Does the condemned man request a last meal?" Only the blindfold was missing.

I called the answering machine and punched in the code.

Beep.

"Jack, we've got a strike to work. We need an operations manager to hire, do the schedules, arrange for cars, radios, everything. Big company, lots of money. Call." It was a friend, Bob Leger, from the City Detective Agency.

Beep.

"I've got a talk show in New York on Friday, next week. We've got a limo. I need a bodyguard, and don't send the stiff from last time, please, Jack?" Laurie Cabot, the official witch of Salem requested.

Beep.

"Hey Jack, you owe me twenty from the Dallas game, sucker!" My friend Wiley said.

Beep.

"We still playing poker Monday night? I got two brand new decks of cards, and Ira is bringing a case of Sam Adams beer. See ya Monday night," my friend Andy said.

Beep.

"Jack? Gordon Little, from WBZ-TV, please call back," a reporter from a local television station said.

Beep.

"Hey, about that midget, they got called to the apartment he lived in tonight, in Revere, and the place had been ripped apart, a total mess, man. And, oh yeah, the M.E. fixed the time of death for the little guy at about 2 a.m. something, about the same time as Ms. Pavoni. Keep your chin up." It was Jim Watson.

I returned to my booth where Ed and one of the strippers, April Waters, were sitting. April was saying how she loved the way Ginger was moving, on stage. "She's so artistic." April sighed.

I glanced up on stage and Ginger was humping a brass fire pole. I looked at Ed and rolled my eyes.

"Look, Jack…maybe you should get out of town for a while, let the cops figure this out. Then when you're out of town and the next stiff shows up, you're in the clear!" But I wasn't running.

"Ed, you been watching cowboy movies on late night television again, haven't you? Why don't you read a book once in a while? A mind is a terrible thing to waste. If you'd have stayed awake longer and watched the rest of that cowboy movie you would have heard the innocent guy say, 'But if I try to leave, they'll think I'm guilty. I gotta stay and fight this out, pardner.'"

As Ed left to return to the bar, I added, "How 'bout a scotch for the road, pardner?"

April asked me if I was in some kind of trouble. I told her it was just a snafu, a merry mix up, a misinterpretation, the wrong place at the wrong time. She looked more confused than ever, and said "Yeah, that happens to me all the time."

April was a young, athletic, raven-haired beauty, and I liked her, even though it took her two hours to watch "60 Minutes."

Ed had returned with a scotch, a beer, and a bouncer. The bouncer said to me, "The man you had, ah, that slight altercation with…he's sitting in a black car parked across the street, a couple of cars back. Two guys sitting in the back seat. There's another that got out of his car. That guy's standing in a doorway on Tremont." The faithful and loyal bouncer returned to his post.

"Christ, to invade a man's sacred ground! To cross the holy boundaries of civilization! To press their totalitarian, bullying, strong-arm tactics in this fine neighborhood is insufferable," I stammered in my finest Richard Burton. Both Ed and April were staring at me, wide-eyed, and mouths open.

"Come on," I said, "where's your spirit of adventure?"

Ed gave me the news. "Jack, you're drunk. April, take him out the stage door, into the van, and over to the Bradford when you pick up the next shift."

To my bewilderment I was escorted behind the stage, through a dressing room of scantily clad heavenly bodies, out a stage door, and into the back of a van. April got in beside me, then five more ladies and a male driver.

The Bradford Hotel was in the same part of town, just four or five blocks from the club. The driver drove under the hotel to the parking garage. We all took the elevator up to the suites the Naked i kept for "international" and traveling exotic dancers on the tenth floor. April and I ended up in her suite.

She asked me to make myself at home so I got some jazz on the radio, made myself a drink, and took off my coat and tie.

April had put on a robe and washed all the makeup off her face. Under that thick veneer of makeup was a pretty girl. As she stood at the mirror, swaying to the jazz and combing out her long black hair, I couldn't believe how wholesome she looked. Like a schoolgirl. She looked like she couldn't have been more than nineteen.

"Where are you from, April?"

"The Midwest, Indiana, and I lived with my Grandma in Minnesota for a while. Why?"

"Well, it's just...I've never looked at you like this before. Like I knew you."

"Jack, you did know me, we had this same conversation before. We stayed together in your office, New Year's Eve." She came over next to me and put her head on my shoulder.

"You're always so preoccupied. You know while I was on stage dancing, I saw you put your gun down, between that guy's legs."

"Yeah, a man don't want to loose his willy, his Johnson, the joystick, Mr. Happy, the one eyed trouser snake, little Peter and the twins, the love gun." Yes, I was drunk.

Being with April in this safe place was a respite for my soul, a recess from the confusion of events. There were still sparks between us, and the electricity drew us together.

"I'm going to make you forget everything for a while, you wild gunslinger. I'm going to release you from all your troubles. And don't make me spank you!"

She proceeded to slowly...release me from all my troubles.

CHAPTER 8

The Dream

I swear I have this dream. It's that some day, I own and operate a nightclub, called "Johnny's". John is my real given name. It's a daydream, but I also dream I'm there at night. It's like a serial dream. I was dreaming now.

The angel had released me and I was at "Johnny's Blues and Jazz Club." The night was humid. One of those hot, steamy, Indian Summer jazz nights. All of the elements were coming together, resulting in a low buzz of animal attraction, in this smoky snake pit known as Johnny's.

Maybe it was the music. The jungle beat. The magic that flows and drifts through the club, out the doors, and up the streets, until it blends together in a tapestry of sound. The backdrop...the soundtrack...to Johnny's place.

The house jazz band was on stage, and the lead cat was playing some dreamy sax lead. There was a cool bass line thumping the room and just the right amount of drums simmering underneath. Glasses were clinking, the conversation level was at a low buzz, and the cash register was ringing and humming steadily in the background.

The indirect lighting was a soft glow and beamed down onto intimate tables and booths. There were old photos of boxing matches featuring local talent, from Rocky Marciano to Marvin Hagler. There were pictures of Boston Celtics, Boston Red Sox, Boston Bruins, and New England Patriot games, mixed with blues and jazz greats, hanging on the walls.

Things were running smoothly as always. I made a little chatter here and bought a few drinks there. The place was cookin'. I sat at the dark end of the bar. I was talkin' with my bartender Jim about painting the outside of the club dark blue. Maybe we'll beef up the central air for the next summer. Now I'm lighting a fine cigar and waiting for the horn band from out of town to finish tuning up and start their set. Yeah, I think I'll put in a few hours workin' the club tonight. I'm relaxing. I'm smoking my Royal Jamaica cigar…I'm adding up the take…I'm payin' out the bands…I do the hiring and firing. At Johnny's place.

"I'll have an Absolut White Russian tonight, Jimmy."

CHAPTER 9

The Book

The next day it was back on the case, and back to the office. What was this item Bob wanted. If it was the money Bella shoved in my pocket, why didn't he just say so? If the cheap heavy was working for the Enormous One, I don't think the roll of hundreds was it. Maybe it was "the book" they were after. The small man that was dropped off at my office in a cardboard box had his apartment ransacked. Somebody was looking for something.

I was staring out my office window to the street four floors below, trying to sort things out, idly watching as a tow truck driver hooked up some poor slob's car. It was the ostentatious pink Cadillac that had been parked there for days. I was thinking what a surprise the owner of the Caddy was going to get when he gets back and his big pink ride was gone. Maybe its' Elvis Presley's' Cadillac.

Then it hit me. What if the owner was dead? How had Bella Pavoni gotten to my office that night? It had been less than a week ago. That could be her car, with four days of tickets stuck on the windshield.

Hadn't Bella dropped some keys here in the office when she tried to pull that gun? I got down and crawled across the floor. They were by the leg of my desk. One set of keys. One of them was pink, and it looked like a car key. There was a pink lucky rabbit's foot attached. I couldn't help but think the foot wasn't lucky for the rabbit or Bella Pavoni.

I ran to the stairs, down to the street, and out the door, but the tow truck was gone. I ran south a block and cut east for two, and I saw the truck going into the South Station tunnel with the pink Cadillac in tow. On the side of the truck was "SOUTHIE TOWING." I knew the place. It was only about twelve blocks away. As the tunnel swallowed up the tow truck, I kept walking at a brisk pace. Over the

Fort Point Channel bridge, past the old Boston Tea Party Ship, the Big Milk Bottle ice cream stand, another block, and there it was.

The pink Cadillac wasn't even off the hook yet. I went into the garage office. As the tow truck driver finished his paperwork and headed back toward the Caddy, I waved the set of keys. "Wait, the Cadillac."

The garage manager, from behind the counter, said, "It's still going to cost you sixty five dollars. As soon as we move it on the street, pal."

"Well, as much as I wish it were mine, it's not. The car belongs to my secretary, Mrs. Pavoni. I just need my economics book from the car to teach my class at the university."

The grease monkey looked me up and down, and I was beginning to think my little pretext was a bit thin, when he said, "I don't know, you seem like a nice enough guy, but, ah, we got a business to run here pal, and, ah, this would be highly irregular…"

I caught his drift. He wanted a little green, the jack, the scratch, the berries, some sugar. I shoved a folded twenty-dollar bill toward him. "I've got to have my lesson books to each the course this evening. I've got thirty-two university students. I have the keys."

"Go ahead, Professor. I'm all for education, and we've all got to do our part. Just leave the keys."

I walked to the pink Cadillac. I didn't know if there was a book in the car, or where it might be, but I'd just paid twenty bucks for the chance to find out. I wanted to find something worth the money. The pink key unlocked the door. Nothing on the seats. Or the glove box. The tow truck driver was watching me, and I didn't want to make it seem like I was rifling the car. I shook my head and mumbled, "Where the hell did she put it? Damned women."

From under the driver's seat, I pulled out a black leather ledger. I gave it a quick flip through the pages. All I saw were numbers and columns of numbers. The tow truck driver was still looking at me quizzically.

"Yes. This is it. The book…to teach the class. Oh, those students will be glad now. Facts and figures. Yes, sir. They're all in here. Like to see you in my night class, fella! Well, thanks," I said tossing the tow truck driver the keys as I began to walk away.

Johnny Barnes

I didn't know if what I had was the book, but my little twenty-dollar ruse had gone far enough. I started walking back towards my office. But I soon realized I couldn't go there. The Garbage Man was looking for me and thought I had "the item." Maybe now I did.

I needed time to check this out. Maybe an accountant could tell me what these numbers and columns meant. I took a cab from South Station to Beacon Hill, to the apartment of Joe Panetta, an accountant who juggles books for the Italian restaurants.

CHAPTER 10

The Bean Counter

Joe Panetta adjusted his glasses, scratched his round belly, and ran his fingers through his silver hair as we talked in his third-floor apartment on Beacon Hill.

"It looks like a duplicate set of books, but there's more than one," Joe said after an hour of study.

"You mean, like a business has one set of books for the IRS, and another for actual costs?"

"Well, there are a lot of reasons for duplicate books. To hide profits from the IRS, or hide employees from the Department of Labor. One owner could present a duplicate set to another owner. A manager might show inflated costs to an out-of-town owner, union reps, Immigration, or to any regulating or governing body, but it's always to hide the actual costs, or some other factor. Like to the IRS, let's say, they'll show a set of books that show high expenses and low profits. But to a prospective owner, they'd show a set of books with low expenses, and a high profit."

"Well, what kind of books do we have here, Joe?"

"It's a little odd. This ledger has two sets of books. One may be the actual, and one may be the altered. But no one ever puts both sets in the same ledger!"

"Not unless they want to show the books are crooked. Not unless they are gathering evidence to show fraud. Or to blackmail someone. What kind of business are we talking about here, Joe?"

"I haven't narrowed that down yet, but by the size of these numbers, it may be contracts. Large contracts, pulling in large figures on a regular basis. I'll look them over some more in the morning, if I could."

"Yeah, sure, Joe. It's getting' late. Look, I gotta tell you, I think at least two people have been killed because they may have had this book, and I know they're after me now. If anything happens to me, make sure Sergeant Jim Watson gets this at the BPD—and be careful. I'll call you."

I put up my collar and walked down the narrow streets of Beacon Hill and disappeared into the dark and rainy Boston night. I felt a little guilty about leaving such a dangerous item with Joe the Bean Counter. I didn't want to suck anybody else into the black hole of trouble that seemed to be following me lately.

I knew there were predators out looking for me. I was hot. If they found me, I could end up in a box like the midget, or with my neck snapped and twisted around like Bella Pavoni's. But it was Monday night, and after supper, I went to the Regular Rotating Super-Secret Monday Night Poker Game me and some of the other guys had. Tonight's game was at Cooper's loft on South Street between Chinatown and Southie. Once again, I found myself in need of a distraction, and thought maybe a poker game with some old friends would fill the bill.

When I got there, the Monday Night Football game had just started. The beer was cold and the poker game was underway. I cracked a cold one and pulled a chair up to the table. I made a twenty-dollar bet with one of the guys, Wiley the Musician, on the Dallas-San Francisco game, taking San Francisco by three.

Wiley said, "San Francisco? What losers. Did you see them against the Giants? No defense. They won't make it to the Super Bowl."

Wiley is an old friend and I knew he was just trying to get me going. I didn't say a word other than "Deal me in."

"Jack, wanna hear the joke of the day?"

"No," was my response, but Wiley went right on.

"A nun gets into a cab and the cabdriver won't stop staring at her. She asks him why he is staring and he replies, 'I have a question to ask you but I don't want to offend you.'

"She answers, 'My dear son, you cannot offend me. When you're as old as I am and have been a nun as long as I have, you get a chance to see and hear just about everything. I'm sure that there's nothing you could say or ask that I would find offensive.'

"Well, I've always had a fantasy to have a nun perform oral sex on me.'

"She responds, 'Well, let's see what we can do about that, but, first you have to be single and second, you must be Catholic.'

"The cab driver is very excited and says, 'Yes, I am single and I'm Catholic too!'

"The nun says, 'O.K., pull into the next alley.'

"He does and the nun fulfills his fantasy. But when they get back on the road, the cab driver starts crying.

"'My dear child, why are you crying?'

"'Forgive me sister, but I have sinned. I lied, I must confess, I'm married and I'm Jewish.'

"The nun says, 'Cry no more...for I have lied too. My name is Kevin and I'm on my way to a Halloween Party.'"

I was kicking back, trying to chill out, but things were happening to me at a faster rate than I could assimilate. It was one thing being set up for a murder rap, with the police looking at me, but now there were people out there who would do me harm, grave harm...and all for a book.

Maybe I should give it up, give it to them, or maybe I should give it to the cops. It was evidence. They would log it, tag it, put it inside an evidence envelope, then put it in a locker in the evidence room in the basement—where it would sit. I needed some time to figure out what it was. Nobody was going to save my ass but me.

The poker game broke up early, about 3 a.m., and Cooper threw me a blanket before he went to his room. Cooper's loft was his home, his photography studio, and his dark room. This was similar to the arrangement I had, converting my office to sleeping quarters at night. Cooper was a blues guitarist who worked as a freelance photographer to help pay the bills.

I was glad just to be somewhere safe where nobody knew I was. I drifted off on the couch with the television on, like it was a night-light, casting shadows on the walls and ceiling, chattering away, oblivious, a tale told by an idiot, signifying nothing.

I was trying to drift off towards the nightclub of my dreams, Johnny's Blues and Jazz Club. I was straining to hear the distant sax. If I could just hear the sax playing, I could walk in that direction. I wanted to be with old friends, wanted to hear the clinking of glasses and the register drawer opening and closing. The tinkling sound of dimes, the clank of quarters, and the crisp sound of paper money being counted out.

But this dream began the way it always did. My feet felt like they were stuck in mud. My thoughts became thick and slow. I soon became aware of something moving in the mud, tracking me, getting closer.

It could sense me. I was in its world now…and it kept on coming, following a trail in the dark towards me as I tried to walk in my sleep.

I was trying to run in the dark, trying to escape, but I felt like I was wearing cement shoes. I could smell the ocean in the distance, but the way was getting thicker with underbrush as evening rapidly approached and darkness began to fall.

It was tracking me, relentless, single minded, and moving closer and closer, shortening the distance between itself and me. The more I struggled the more it enjoyed hunting me.

Johnny Barnes

As I struggled to make my way to the ocean's edge, my progress became slower and slower—the harder I tried to move the more bogged down I became. It was getting closer and closer…

I strained to pick up each leg and move forward even as I sensed it coming up behind me. I could hear the brush crunching under its weight. I could smell the foul stench of it coming up behind me.

As I gathered all my strength for a final burst of effort, I heard a slow hissing sound behind me, growing louder and louder, building to a crescendo in a roar of hedonistic glee. I was about to be ravaged and consumed.

The roar was ear splitting now and I could feel it's hot breath on my back, the stench sickened me. As I turned slowly and fearfully to look at my fate, I awoke in a cold sweat.

CHAPTER 11

We Have Nothing To Fear

I awoke with an enormous hangover the size of the Boston Public Library. After a shower, three aspirin tablets, some tomato juice, and Tabasco sauce with a raw egg, I was on the phone to Joe Panetta, the Bean Counter.

"I think you might be right about this set of books, Jack. It looks like somebody has both sets of books in this one ledger. And parts are highlighted to show major discrepancies. There are two distinct sets of books, and one doesn't square with the other. What's strange, though, is that there are no company names, just an assigned number. In the back of the ledger is a list of numbers. I think it's a code for all the businesses in the books."

71

"Blackmail, that's the name of the game. Nice work, Joe. How long before you crack the code?"

"No telling that, Jack. I may not be able to, depending on how complex it is. But it might be simple. Things may click, depending on how much the books were designed to show. I'll look."

"Thanks. This may be important."

"This puzzle is fascinating, Jack. I'm hooked. I'll check it out. Call me tonight?"

"Yeah. Hey, Joe, don't let anyone know what you're working on, okay? And watch your back."

My suspicions were correct. Somebody was set to blackmail the Fat Man and his company. If this was his book, and he was being blackmailed, he may have been driven to kill. Maybe he was a guy who had a lot to lose. A very large guy who had gone from poor to rich. A big guy with friends in high places. An enormous guy who had everything to lose and would get a jail term tacked on for good measure. A huge man whose lifestyle and physical requirements just didn't fit in with the prison regimen. He might kill. I don't know what I'd do under those circumstances. Could you order a hit from your leather chair, from your condo overlooking Boston and the Harbor? The Huge One may not have had to wash any blood from his hands, but he still smelled like garbage.

I'll have to bang the phone from Cooper's loft, I couldn't let Bob and his goon squad get on my tail, but I needed to work the streets. I'm a detective. It's what I do. I needed to get somebody talking. The local code of silence is over rated. Omerta. People loved to talk. They'd go on all day. When I was a cop, co-conspirators would talk to make a deal. We called it "dry snitching." It meant the rat stayed off the witness stand.

Before I started working the phone, I went down to the corner store for some supplies—orange juice, milk, cereal, and some hot coffee. I got the newspaper, two cheap cigars, and I was set for the day.

I returned to Cooper's loft and picked up the phone to make a call to my answering machine. I opened the paper and saw the headline: "8TH VICTIM FOUND-CITY IN PANIC!"

Christ! Somebody was killing people, and they had to get nailed soon. How could someone commit eight murders and not leave evidence and clues for the cops? I wished I still had the resources of the city's police department. I would be combing the crime scenes for forensic evidence, rattling cages, shaking the bushes. Detectives would be working the street. Pumping their sources. Calling in favors. Digging deep and coming up with answers. Yeah, that's what detectives do.

But I'm pretty much alone on this one, and we'll have to see what one lonely private detective can do.

At times like this, I wondered why I'd wanted to be a detective since I was five years old. In college I'd majored in Philosophy instead of law enforcement. From Aristotle's metaphysics to Zen Buddhism. I loved those wacky philosophers.

Socrates, Plato, Nietzsche, Descartes, Divinci, Buddha, even Meher Baba. In his simplistic way, Meher Baba said "Don't worry, be happy." Yeah, don't worry, be happy, and in this modern time, violence will enter your world and shatter everything you hold sacred. After I got out of college, I checked the classifieds and soon found out there were no jobs for philosophers.

I called my answering machine as I turned to the article on the serial killing.

"Hey, bad boy, you gonna visit me tonight?" my girlfriend said.

Beep. "Jack? Watson here. I'm still on my fishing trip, stopped at a pay phone in Edgartown, on the Vineyard. I called Bill Rogers at the Homicide Unit on a different matter, and he started asking me where you might be. He asked if I knew where you were last night, and said too bad you weren't with me. He said the State Police, all of a sudden, are pressing for an arrest, and they're going to come in. The Lieutenant Governor sent them. The state investigators mentioned your name to Rogers. Holy Christ, Jack. See you in a couple of days."

I was in shock. I hung up the phone and turned to the newspaper article. I half expected to see my picture in the paper with the caption "HAVE YOU SEEN THIS MAN?"

The article was short. The latest and eighth victim was found by a boater as he walked his dog on the shore by the piers. He'd found the body in the fog at 4:15 a.m. It was propped up in a sitting position, his back leaning on a pylon at the end of Pier 4. His neck was broken.

There were other signs of physical abuse. No witnesses. No obvious clues.

With the addition of the midget, this made it eight. The deceased, Henri Riley, aged fifty-one, lived in suburbia, worked downtown, and was an accountant for the state. Another bean counter.

Why were the cops looking at me? It wouldn't be the first time the area cops would rush to judgement. I felt a tightness around my neck and throat, and it was a little harder to swallow. I hoped they had some leads in another direction. I hadn't paid much attention to the first couple of murders—Boston routinely had a couple a week. I hadn't bought into the serial killer theory at first, not until after the third or fourth killing. But the murders now had my full attention.

I wondered how that would look on my resume—Suspected Serial Killer.

CHAPTER 12

Suspected Serial Killer

I wondered where it was going to stop. At least seven for Jack the Ripper. Jeffrey Dahmer had 16. Elmer Henley had 27. John Wayne Gacey 33. Ted Bundy had 40. The Green River Murderer 46 plus, unsolved. Henry Lucas confessed to 188 murders in twenty-four states.

I checked my office answering machine again at noon. Sergeant Bill Rogers had called and mentioned very casually he'd like me to give him a "jingle" at the Homicide Division. "Just some follow-up."

Another day, and I was getting in deeper and deeper instead of digging my way out. While I was sleeping, someone was creeping. While I was dreaming, someone was scheming. While I was napping,

77

someone was capping, another victim. At least today's dead body didn't have my business card in his pocket. I hoped.

I was beginning to feel trapped, boxed in. I couldn't run, and I couldn't be seen on the streets by the goons who worked for Fat Boy. Police protection was out of the question. They were looking for me, too.

I needed a plan. Someone was working overtime to slam me, one way or the other, just for that book. At least I really did have it now. Well, I could get it, although I wasn't quite sure what it was.

After a few more minutes of feeling sorry for myself, accompanied by moanings of "Why me?," I took a cab to the Boston Public Library to do some research.

The massive BPL, on Boylston Street in the Back Bay, was quiet on this school day. I could be wrong but I doubted if any of the Garbage Man's goon squad frequented the library. On the third floor, in the back of the library, there was a section for viewing microfilm. All of the Boston Globes for the last many years were on these microfilms. Most all of the serious reported local crimes and especially homicides, were either on the front page, or on the front page of the "Metro" section of the Globe. It was possible to scan through a month of Boston Globes in a few minutes on a microfilm viewer. Or I could get some computer time and access the Internet with its search engines. In the past I'd worked this angle on a lot of cases. Missing person (obituaries), articles beginning with "Body Found...," tracing criminal careers, following cases I'd been working on, and catching up on cases I came to late. Those investigative reporters do a great job.

The serial killings had begun about four months before, I recalled. I ran the microfilm from six months back and found nothing. Five months showed the same, as did four months and three. Two months...and there it was.

"BODY FOUND-MAY BE WORK OF SERIAL KILLER." The article went on to say police sources said the first body, found floating in Boston Harbor five weeks before, had links to two other homicide victims found in the area. All three had signs of physical abuse, as well as brutally broken necks.

The first body was that of James Pendergast, age thirty-nine. He was captain of the "Northsea," a charter fishing boat he lived on.

Captain Pendergast was found in Boston Harbor floating by the docks, several hundred yards from his boat. It was first thought he had fallen off his boat, breaking his neck on the way down into the water where he had drowned. It had since been determined Captain Pendergast's vessel had been ransacked and his neck had been broken an hour before he entered the water.

The second victim was Rick O'Hare, the thirty-six-year-old manager of The Channel, a nightclub on the waterfront with ties to organized crime. He was found in the employee parking lot outside the club next to his car at 3:45 a.m. with a broken neck. O'Hare also lived on board the Northsea, docked near Pier 4, with Capt. Pendergast.

The third victim, was Paul Moreau, a forty-seven-year-old accountant. It was later determined that his neck had been broken before being thrown off the Mystic Tobin Bridge. He was found floating under the bridge in Boston Harbor. It was first believed he had jumped from the famous leap above, where Charles Stuart jumped to his death on January 4, 1990 after being implicated in the murder of his wife, in a crime that shocked the nation. Stuart had blamed the Mission Hill shooting death of his wife and unborn child on a black robber. The police and good people of Boston, seemed to some, to be a little too willing to believe that a black man with a criminal record had shot the middle-class white couple who were in the wrong neighborhood late at night.

I made copies of the Globe article before the library closed and headed out into the rain. I wanted to read about the other murders, but it would have to wait. The sky was getting dark. I needed supper, a shower, and the company of my girlfriend. I called her from Friday's, a bar on Newbury Street, and told her to meet me at the restaurant where we had our first date. I told her to take a cab and to get out three blocks from the restaurant, and to make sure she wasn't followed.

She arrived at Friday's about an hour later. After we ordered some drinks and appetizers, she asked me what all the intrigue was about this time. I told her I just wanted to see if she remembered where our first date was.

"Come on, Jack, you knew I would remember that. You're really scared about something, aren't you? Just tell me who is bothering you, and I'll make them go away."

God, she was good to look at—sophisticated, warm, and sensitive. That long brown hair and those big green eyes. Attractive, intelligent, levelheaded. A classic. It was easy to see why I loved her and needed her.

Over the next two hours, I told her everything that had happened. At times she stopped eating and stared at me, wide-eyed. At other times she shook her head in disbelief. Many women would've walked away.

"What are we going to do, Jack?" she said.

"Well, tonight we're going to a hotel."

She loved to go to a hotel—it was an aphrodisiac to her. She brightened up at the prospect. I didn't think she realized the gravity of my situation.

We took a cab to the Haymarket area, then walked over to the Bostonian Hotel, where I had been the house detective after I'd first left the force. The Bostonian was sold out, but they always kept a few rooms open for "friends of the hotel."

The room was beautiful, with a view overlooking the Italian North End, the shops of the Haymarket and Faneuil Hall, and with a downtown Boston skyline. It had a sunken Jacuzzi, and a big bed. I located a jazz station on the radio, and we ordered some drinks from room service. We ended up in the hot tub, and it felt great. We drank, I lit a cigar, and we made small talk while her toes began to tickle me underneath the bubbles.

"Oh, baby, sometimes I wish I could get that nightclub, and put it on an island, like Martha's Vineyard. I wouldn't even care if anybody came in or not," I told her. I kept on talking and talking.

"Now, here I've been talking about myself all night. Maybe I'm just too self-centered. Do you think I'm too self-centered? I won't talk about myself anymore tonight. In fact, I'd rather listen to you. So tell me, what do you like about me?"

We laughed, and then didn't speak again that night.

Johnny Barnes

We moved to the bed and made love. It felt good to lie in her arms. I felt safe, like a baby. Maybe she could make them all go away. Maybe she was right, I was scared.

CHAPTER 13

Good Dreams

As I drifted off to sleep, I heard the echo of a saxophone riffing in the distance. A cool bass was walking through its' progressions. Jazz. Sleepy jazz, blowing down the streets, through the alleys, up the tenements, around the buildings, and over the rooftops. I walked towards the sound. Down one more street, around the corner, and I was there.

Johnny's Blues and Jazz Club. I was more than welcome. Man, I owned the place. I knew most of the fine local clientele, and those I didn't know, knew me. Under colored lights, jazz was flowing from the house band. The drinks were flowing from the bar, and cash was flowing back into the registers. The American Dream. Yeah, this was it all right.

I took up a spot down at the end of the bar. My bartender, James, gave me a Jamaica Royal cigar and got me a bottle of Beaujolais from a case I keep in the storeroom. The place was doing well tonight. In attendance were some celebrities, sports stars, media people, musicians, and lots of beautiful women, with whom I had several deep conversations about life, love, sex, music, and art. The little head started doing the thinking for the big head, and I ended up in my office behind the stage with the new waitress. Then it was over like a summer shower…all that was left was wet and dripping. This dream was going well.

After she left I sank back into the leather couch and began to doze off. I remember sinking into the couch and beginning to drift. I remember thinking, how could I dream, if I was already asleep and dreaming? How can I dream about Johnny's nightclub, if I'm already there?

CHAPTER 14

Bad Dreams

I was standing in the woods. It was dark, except for the moonlight. I was listening. I heard something moving towards me in the distance. I looked around, but the surroundings were unfamiliar. I knew I had to move out, but I wasn't sure in which direction. I began to run as the stalker proceeded to track me. I ran through woods, fields, streams, and over rocks. My legs grew heavier and my feet felt like they were stuck in mud. I tried to lose The Tracker by changing direction, but it kept coming after me.

Whatever it was, it knew me. It zigged when I zigged, zagged when I zagged. It was relentless. It was as merciless as a hungry shark. As cold as a snake…I reached the cliffs overlooking the Atlantic, and I could run no further.

My body shook as I turned to meet the onrushing tracker…and slap! Something hit me on the side of my face. And again. Slap!

"Jack! Jack!"

I struggled to open my eyes, and saw my girlfriend looking over me from the bed. I was on the floor.

"Jesus Christ, Jack! You were shaking and moaning and fell off the bed."

I was startled, and it took a moment to orient myself from the slap of reality.

"Shaking? Moaning?" I said. "Sounds like good sex."

"Oh Jack! You're so immature!" she said, and pulled the covers back over her head.

"I can only be young once, but I can be immature all my life," I said as I slid back up onto the bed.

CHAPTER 15

A Room With a View

I had her go down and get the newspaper in the morning—I didn't know if my face was going to be on the front page or not. I was going back to work today. More of the puzzle might be filled in if I went back to the Boston Public Library and scanned the back issues of the newspapers. I also needed to check with the county assessor's office and see what property was owned by Mr. Big. I was afraid to call my answering machine.

She came back a few minutes later, told me my picture was not in the paper, dropped two newspapers on the bed, and left for her job teaching kindergarten.

I began to read the paper over as I ate my room service breakfast. On page three, there was some follow-up on the killings. Henri Riley was the eighth victim, found sitting at the end of Pier 4 the night before last. He was an accountant for the Special Investigations Unit of the State of Massachusetts. The District Attorney was quoted as saying the State Police, with the assistance of the FBI, would be channeling their resources to the case, and an arrest was eminent. When asked if there was a suspect, the DA stated, "We are collecting evidence, interviewing any relevant parties, and the FBI is constructing a psychological profile of the serial killer. No monster can prey upon the citizens of Greater Boston and get away with it!"

It must be an election year.

I flipped through the paper, looking for the Las Vegas line on the week's football games. I landed instead on the obituary page. There was a picture of Henri Riley, the latest victim of the serial killer. He looked like a real human being—fairly innocuous in appearance, early fifties, gray hair, and glasses. He left a wife, three daughters, and eleven grandchildren.

The obituary also stated "Hank" Riley was an accountant for the Special Investigation Unit for the state. They handled fraud cases, worker compensation cases, and state government scams, frauds, and "discrepancies." I wondered if somebody like that would be interested in seeing the book.

I called my brother, the attorney. He had been reading the papers, but couldn't understand how I could be involved. I wasn't involved, I protested. My brother urged me to turn myself in. I'm not officially wanted, I protested again. He just couldn't understand that I could be the only one in a position to figure out who was behind all this. I couldn't do anything from an interview room at the Criminal Investigations Division downtown. My brother promised he would give it his "undivided attention" as soon as I was charged with something.

I wondered if the phrase "the attorney who represents himself has a fool for a client" was applicable to a sibling.

I called Joe Panetta, the Bean Counter, at his office. He couldn't tell me much, other than the fact that the size of the numbers in the book were very large. One gross take for the year—approximately sixty-five million dollars. That's a very large figure, to me. It's a large figure to some small nations.

I called the dreaded answering machine. The first, and only call on the machine was a sinister, electronically altered voice that sounded like a garbage disposal. "You went to the pink car, didn't you? I know you have it. This matter is most urgent. We can work something out."

A chill ran up my spine like somebody had walked over my grave. I was getting in deeper and deeper. I was hotter than a hen in a barn full of roosters. I had the press looking for me, the Boston Police, the State Police with the assistance of the FBI, and Psycho Blimp and his goon squad. The roll of $100 bills Bella Pavoni had stuck down my pants had shrunk, along with the rest of the equipment down there. I had thought I was getting easy money…money for nothing.

For the time being, I felt safe at the Bostonian Hotel. I wasn't officially registered as a guest at the front desk. Just to make sure the staff understood, I went down to the desk and told the house detective, the bell captain, and the front desk attendant, I was laying low because a client's husband was a bit irate. In other words, if anybody was looking for me, I wasn't there. But in the back of my mind, I knew I had to go deeper underground. I hopped in a cab and headed for the county assessor's office for more research.

Thaddeus Reno owned a lot of property. He had garages and parking lots in Southie and Boston, where he kept and maintained his fleet of garbage trucks. He had some valuable vacant waterfront land near Pier 4. Reno owned the town house on Admiral's Hill in Chelsea, at 80 Captains Row, where he lives. He owned the three-decker in Bay Village where he was born, which now houses a fag bar. I mean gay club. I'm a sensitive, caring, politically correct person.

I took a cab and drove past his town house in Chelsea. It gave me a sense of power to drive by the Heavy Ones' home. I knew where he lived. It was small satisfaction for someone who had been in the dark with the world closing in around him.

I had to make some connection between Reno's victims and the serial killer's victims besides the broken necks. Were the serial killings some kind of smoke screen? And what did it have to do with me?

I had the cab driver take me back over the Mystic River Bridge, passing the U.S.S. Constitution, Old Ironsides, whose masts and rigging jut out in front of the Boston skyline, and asked him to drop me at the Boston Public Library. There were other victims of the serial killer I had to get to know.

The newspaper microfilm section was quiet and peaceful. I couldn't help but think how impossible it would be for me to conduct the investigation from a jail cell...or from underneath a ton of Boston garbage at the city landfill.

After about twenty-five minutes of viewing the microfilms, I found some follow-up information on the third victim, Paul Moreau, the accountant. He'd been found floating under the Mystic Tobin Bridge after having been thrown off with his neck broken. He had been dead for a week. It seemed he also did real estate work for a wealthy Boston family, the Pavonis of Beacon and Chestnut Hills, as well as being an accountant for Reno Waste Management.

Another article, from two weeks before, had a story on the fourth victim. He was twenty-eight-year-old Gerard Spring, an independent computer analyst. He was found by some kids who were trying to wash his windshield at the red light on A Street and Broadway in Southie. The kids started washing his windshield, where he was parked sitting in his car, engine still running, and staring straight ahead. Then they asked him for a dollar. When one of the urchins reached in the open window and touched his shoulder, he slumped forward, his forehead hitting the steering wheel and sounding the horn. When they realized he was dead, the kids had gone screaming out of the neighborhood. It took the cops two hours to round them up. Mr. Spring's neck had been broken like a Nebraska farm chicken on Sunday morning.

The fifth victim seemed to be a real fly in the ointment. He was a tall, thin guy, with long blond hair. He was about twenty-four years old. His name was Digby Riggs—one of his names. He went by several, according to the Globe. Digby Riggs was a recording star with CSB Records. He played rock and roll with his Boston based-band in all the clubs around town, and sometimes went on tour. The name on his driver's license was Robert Black. He was also known as Kim French when he performed in drag queen splendor at local bars in the notorious Bay Village section of Beantown.

He was found at the end of runway 14-32 at Logan International Airport. A lobsterman putting out his traps in the harbor discovered the eerie sight by the airport as the sun came up. Mr. Riggs was propped up in a standing position at the end of the runway, tied up like a scarecrow to a marker light pole, dressed in drag. With his long blond hair, thick red lipstick, blush, eyeliner, and full make-up. He had earrings the size of small chandeliers dripping to his shoulders. His light blue strapless chiffon gown was blowing gently in the morning breeze.

Occasionally a DC-10 would overshoot a runway and dump a few bodies into Boston Harbor, but this serial killer liked to display his work.

The library was closing, and the last rays of sunlight hit the tops of the taller Boston skyscrapers, the Prudential and the Hancock, even as a sudden cloudburst was passing through. I had a lot to think about. I pulled my hat down, my collar up, and walked across town by back streets and alleys.

Traffic was heavy. I walked from the cigar store on Massachusetts Avenue up Newbury Street to the Boston Public

Gardens and the Boston Common, then over Beacon Hill, avoiding the Combat Zone, and through Government Center. I headed down along the back streets of downtown, through the Leather District, and to the waterfront.

I ended up at Pier 4. The rain had passed and the skies were clearing. An eerie mist rolled in as I walked out towards the end of the pier. It was getting dark fast. The backdrop of city lights began to dominate the skyline. It was breathtaking.

The wind had shifted, and the huge jets coming into Logan were flying what seemed like only a couple of hundred yards over my head as they approached the runways. Each plane's engine made a loud winding down sound as they came in overhead. The jets were stacked up in the distance, each one higher and farther back, like an ascending stairway. Each plane awaiting entry, one approaching every few minutes.

I arrived at the end of the pier and I realized this was where they'd found the eighth victim, Henri Riley, propped up by one of these pilings, his neck snapped. I thought of how his wife, kids, family and friends were dealing with his murder by some twisted freak who liked to snap necks. His life was no less important than mine, and probably more so, at least to his family and friends.

I could see Admirals' Hill from the pier, and I wondered if Thaddeus Reno was capable of treating a human being like garbage. I could also see the Mystic Tobin Bridge, where Paul Moreau, the accountant who worked for Bella Pavoni's family and Reno, was thrown from after his neck was snapped. My body suddenly went rigid and my thoughts became clear.

In a flash I could see it all. It was a case of where you stand determines what you see. I could see the runways of Logan Airport where the cross-dressing rock and roller, Digby Riggs, was found, and I could see the docks by Atlantic Avenue where Pendergast, the boat captain, was found. I could see the nightclub where Rick O'Hare was found. I could also see the abandoned rail cars where Bella Pavoni stared back at me in horror.

A chill went up and down my spine, and my body shook. I looked back to Admirals' Hill and realized Thaddeus Reno, the garbage man, could see these locations, too.

I imagined him in a front room with a harbor view, sitting alone in an oversized chair, stuffing food in his mouth. Grunting, groaning, and belching in a gastronomical orgy. Licking, sucking, and chewing noisily from trays overflowing with prepared food, and washing it down with tumblers filled with liquids as he looked out over Boston Harbor through a high powered telescope.

CHAPTER 16

Scotch and Reefer

On my way back to the Bostonian, I passed the abandoned rail cars near Pier 4 and Northern Avenue as I walked back into Boston after dark. I could see the town houses of Admirals' Hill rising above the Chelsea side of the Mystic Tobin Bridge from which Paul Moreau, the Reno Waste Management accountant, was thrown. I walked past the pylons by Atlantic Avenue where Captain Pendergast's corpse was found floating. I walked on down Necco Street to the waterfront nightclub, the Channel. It was a huge one-story building, partially built over a channel of water, and surrounded on the other three sides by parking lots. From the picture in the newspaper I knew the parking lot, directly in front of the club, was where one of the serial killer's earlier victims, club manager Rick O'Hare's, twisted body was found, lying between his car and a big, rusty, greasy, blue Dumpster, twenty-five yards from the front door, after locking up the club one night. Who had he seen? Did he know something? Did he have something that belonged to someone else— someone rather large? The huge, industrial-size, blue Dumpster bore silent witness to the crime. The Dumpster with the "ELECT LT. GOV. KING" sticker on it. The Dumpster marked "PROPERTY OF RENO WASTE MANAGEMENT."

From that crime scene, I could look down the two blocks to Broadway and A Streets. This was where the fourth victim, Gerard Spring, the computer hack, was found dead by the Southie kids, sitting in his car at the intersection, engine idling, staring straight ahead. Someone must have been thoughtful enough to twist his head back in the proper direction before leaving him.

I stared back at Admiral's Hill.

I'd always loved those old black and white detective films—film Noir. Dark films. I enjoyed the old detective stories with all the oddball characters—thieves, drunks, night walkers, psycho cops, killers, femme fatales, blackmailers, sexual deviants, the decadent rich, the drastically poor—players motivated by fabulous riches, power games of lust, greed, and dominance. And the detective, working without a net, against the odds.

They didn't make them like that anymore. Sometimes I felt like I was in one of those old movies. But this was all too real—the dark shadows of the city, the back streets and back alley deals, the drugs, booze, prostitution. The thieves and burglars of the night. The quiet stalking. The abuse that goes on behind closed doors. The dark, secret, sex crimes. Love and hate. It hasn't changed since the days of the black and white detective films. And earlier. In every corner of the globe.

I'd found that you had to stand for something...or you'd fall for anything.

People hadn't changed. There was a nation of victims, and a community of perpetrators. As long as the cover of night cloaks our most secret desires, love and violence will sleep in the same bed. And the ultimate crime...murder. The ultimate murderer...the serial killer. The evil human predator that hunts and stalks his victim, to kill and possibly torture. In an act of power and sexual gratification, without a conscience. Fascinated by violence and torture.

This was all too real.

I knew I was too hot to stay at the Bostonian. I had to call my girlfriend and get her out of there, too. I went to the pay phone inside the Channel.

The empty club was cavernous. Although it was just a one-floor building, it was spread over four acres, along the murky Fort Point Channel, between Boston and South Boston. The interior of the club was painted entirely in flat black. The walls, ceiling, and the floor, the bar, everything was flat black. The stage in the back corner was lit up with multicolored spot lighting. A rock band—the sign over the stage read "The Night Crawlers"—were doing a sound check, testing their equipment and going over a few songs.

I managed to speak to her over the wall of sound. She was to clear out of the hotel in the morning, and even if I knew where I would be, I wouldn't tell her. She knew the routine, and this was no fire drill. I told her to watch her ass and I'd be in touch.

Though I thought I might regret it, I checked the answering machine at the office. There was a series of clicks, which meant someone had called in many times, but had hung up when no one answered. Then there was a call from Sergeant Bill Rogers asking me to call him, then a call from Detective Sergeant Jeffrey Houston of the Mass State Police asking me to call him. Then four or five more clicks and a call from WBZ-TV reporter Gordon Little.

As I was about to leave the Channel, I noticed a Reno Waste Management truck out front emptying the Dumpster. I figured it was a good time to hide out at the bar in the VIP lounge in the rear of the nightclub. There was one bartender on duty and two customers, businessman types, in attendance. I ordered a Guinness Stout for supper and got a bowl of popcorn with it. I had to think about my next move anyway, and as I thumbed through the Boston Globe someone had left on the bar, I realized I had no idea what my next move would be.

Three Asian ladies came in and sat at a table right in front of a television showing videos of scantily clad men dancing, or grinding, suggestively. The ladies ordered drinks and began pointing, giggling, and squirming with delight as the men on the television stripped down and flexed their goods. Imagine, reducing those poor men to sex objects for their own immature and puerile gratification. Shocking.

I engaged the bartender in some light banter, mostly about the club, and then asked an offhand question. "Say, didn't I read about a bartender gettin' killed or something here?" A mild look of both mock surprise at my sudden realization and sympathy for the living was expressed on my boyish face.

"Yeah, Rick. Rick O'Hare. The nicest guy you ever wanna meet. He ran this place like we were a family, man. He hired me. Worked together since he came in, almost a year ago. He put in long hours, man. Stayed on a boat right at Pier 4. The North Sea. They found the captain of the boat floating in the harbor. Goddamn shame, man. Rick was like my big brother."

"They get the guy who did it?"

"Well, ain't you been readin' about the serial killer, man? Rick had a snapped neck, just like the others. But I don't know."

"What? You think somebody else?"

He looked around, then leaned forward and whispered.

"Maybe his neck was snapped, but…things were gettin' strange around here, man. Like a certain element was movin' in and slowly takin' over the place, more and more."

At this point, he seemed to realize he was telling a complete stranger more than he ever intended to, and added, "Hey man, I just pour the beer and don't know nothin'."

I ordered another beer, a bowl of popcorn, and tipped the barkeep well. I was wondering if I was in an episode of The Twilight Zone. Everybody knew more of what was going on than I did. I picked up a flyer listing the acts appearing in the back lounge here at the Channel. One act was Kim French, A.k.a. Digby Riggs, drag queen, and the corpse that was found on the airport runway. I pointed to the queen's picture and the bartender nodded.

"He won't be back." What an understatement.

"That's one of the weird acts they were bringin' in, man. We used to be strictly rock and roll, man. Mostly musicians, fans, industry people, groupies. Now we got transvestites singin' Sinatra. Now we got fruit loops hangin' around. Gangsters, Hell's Angels, queens, lesbians, wise guys, man. We even had the Lieutenant Governor here more than a few times. He parks the limo in the alley."

I stared out the window overlooking the moonlit channel that ran in and out with the tide between Southie and Boston. The towering buildings of Boston reminded me of NFL linebackers, hovering over me, waiting for me to call the next play. I felt soon a plan would come to me and the pieces would fall into place, the muddy waters would clear, and I would eventually see.

Or maybe the dark beer was seeping into my thinking.

There had to be some connections. The crime scenes and bodies found had all been in this area—Bella in the abandoned rail car, Rick O'Hare, the club manager, in the parking lot. Pendergast, the boat Captain, the floater in the harbor, Paul Moreau, the accountant for Bella's family and Reno's company, under the bridge, Digby Riggs, had been found across the harbor, on the airport runway. There was Gerard Spring, the computer hack, found just down the street in his car, Henri Riley, the state fraud investigator, at the end of Pier 4. The dead midget, Benny Lopes from New Bedford, had been in a package delivered to my office in nearby Chinatown.

I crossed the channel, walked the five blocks to Cooper's loft on South Street, found the key over the hallway closet, and let myself in. I washed up, made a scotch and soda, flipped on the tube, and settled onto the couch. Some Friday night for the big city detective, but I was glad my old friend Cooper had this big studio loft, where I could kick back from time to time.

Cooper had been married, but he is now a confirmed bachelor. He says he left his wife because she was a terrible cook. For years, after he left her, if he went into a restaurant and the menu said "Home Style Cooking," he left.

Now he ate only from the three basic food groups—take out, frozen, and canned. It was a doomed relationship. She was as hard to get as a close-up of the horizon. And he has been turned down more times than the sheets on a bed at a cheap motel.

Cooper was down on the Cape at a shoot. He was "shootin' Jews," as he called it, when he had a photo assignment for a "grip and grin" at a Jewish ceremony or event. Cooper's family was Jewish, so I guess he could get away with saying that. I wouldn't try it.

He didn't like the "grip and grin" assignments, but after that, he was back to shooting models on a beach, by the hotel pool, or in the studio. I guess things tend to balance out, in the long run.

I wanted to call Bill Rogers at Homicide and tell him there was some connection with the waterfront locations and the murders, but I didn't know what that connection was. Sometimes, there are no connections, even for a serial killer. Many "stranger" murders are committed by undetected killers. Two out of five go unsolved.

I decided not to call Rogers. I didn't want him to tell me to come in, and then not do it, because then I could be considered a fugitive. Besides, Bill worked days, and he probably wouldn't be there anyway. I had to hope the cops were making some progress in their investigation. After all, they were detectives. But I found little solace in that.

By the time I finished a Royal Jamaica cigar with my third scotch and soda, I had jazz on the radio, had turned down the lights, and was settling into the couch, with my blanket and pillow. Cooper, or one of his models, had left half a joint in the ashtray. That's all I needed. The cops would come to pick me up for questioning, they'd find the weed, and in the morning the newspapers would read "DRUG BUST!" "Police swoop down on suspected serial killer last night only to find him in possession of a quantity of contraband, illegal controlled substances. Police were horrified. Suspect's detective agency license is revoked! Suspect held without bail! Estimated street value of the bust $225,362.27."

CHAPTER 17

Red Army Ants

I looked out the window. There was nobody suspicious down on the street. I had to get rid of the reefer. I looked around like some sort of criminal. There was nobody watching. I lit it up. Yeah! If I was going to go down, I was going down big! Panama Red. Reefer Madness. Now I was a criminal.

I smoked that reefer down to a burning flake that drifted through the air, from side to side, and expired before it hit the floor. Then I settled deeper into the couch...and let the jazz do its thing.

Maybe that crack team of investigators down at Homicide would have this all wrapped up with a pretty red bow by the time I woke up.

111

I began to drift, and I began to dream…

I had trouble moving…It was as if I was becoming more and more paralyzed. My thoughts slowed. I could still breathe, move my eyes, and swallow, but my feet were heavy. And my arms wouldn't move. I was dreaming it was a sunny morning and I was sitting in a wooden chair in a one-room cabin. I was sitting very still. I couldn't get up.

Underneath the cabin door, I watched a few red ants march in. Just a few red ants. One by one. Just a thin trickle, sliding under the door, coming into the room. Then a single line of red ants. Then side by side, the line got a bit thicker, and thicker. Then ten across, then twenty. Soon hundreds of red Army Ants began marching in under the closed door in an increasingly wide swath like a blood-red ribbon.

The band widened to a foot wide, then three feet, then four feet across, until thousands of little red ants in a widening strip came streaming in under the door. And they headed for me. Like a wave of moving, living carpet, they spread across the floor.

They were down around my feet now…They began moving up the chair legs, where I sat unable to move, over my feet, and onto my legs…They crawled in and out of my shoes, then inside my pant legs. I was trying not to think about how they felt, crawling on my skin with their tiny little feet. Moving their tiny legs. Taking tiny little steps.

They began to nip a bit but I still couldn't move. They slowly moved up inside my pants and began crawling over my crotch. Several divisions, or squads, began crawling inside my underwear. The army continued on, up onto my stomach and chest. The red Army Ants were swarming over me. The ants were still coming through the door. Under the door, across the floor, up onto my body, covering it, nipping and biting.

I recall reading that ants are the only other living entities on the planet besides humans that wages organized warfare.

Even though I was experiencing an adrenaline rush, resulting from this direct frontal assault, I could not move. I was paralyzed. The red Army Ants crawled and swarmed around my collar and neck. Some began crawling behind my ears. Then in and out of my ears. I could hear their little ant feet crossing my eardrums. Up the back of my neck, and into my hair. Then they began crawling in and out of my nose, down my throat, and across my eyes. The ants were crawling in my mouth, clusters of them. I was spitting and choking.

I woke-up cold and sweating. I was bug eyed and frantically brushing off the imaginary ants.

My dreams seemed to be very good or very bad. I wished I could have mildly pleasant dreams. Middle of the road or above average dreams, like driving a spaceship, hitting a grand slam at Fenway Park, or meeting the president.

No more Red Army Ants.

But if these kinds of activities, these strange dreams of control and powerlessness, are going on in my unconscious mind, what else could be happening? Could I have a dark side I can't remember? Are there both a Dr. Jekyll and a Mr. Hyde within me? A Jack The Ripper? A Boston Strangler? Could I actually be the serial killer? Could I have a major psychological disorder? Am I a bi-polar schizophrenic with multiple personalities? Could I have a twisted, sinister side that takes over and makes me commit murder and unspeakable acts of sin and depravity?...Nah.

CHAPTER 18

Heavy Rain

It was a bright, sunny, morning, a new day, and a new chance to get this monkey off my back. I was still free to dig into this most important case. My client was dead and now I had to defend myself. I wasn't going down for this one.

It was tough talk for a private eye who was in it up to his neck. But I felt good. Something had to give.

I called my accountant sleuth, Joe Panetta.

"Where you been, Jack? I've left two messages on your machine today."

"Never mind that, Joe, you don't want to know. What have you got? You made any more sense out of the book other than it's a duplicate ledger made by someone who wanted to document some kind of…inappropriate fiscal responsibility? I need more. I think this book may be tied to the serial killings, and it's me that may be taking the fall."

I hoped I didn't sound as desperate as I felt, but the Bean Counter was someone I was counting on to help me add things up and get me on track.

"If you'd let me get a word in edgewise, I think I might have something."

"Go ahead."

"The more I looked at the seven-digit numbers in the back of the book, the more I realized they were unusual for bookkeeping standards. My guess is they don't really have any quantitative meaning. The summary proportions don't add up."

"Speak English, Joe."

"It's just an identifier code. It names the clients involved. The contractors. The businesses involved."

"It's a code?"

"Well, yes, but after staring at the numbers for a while, I realized it was a simple code like my secret "Girl Haters Club" code, I used when I was a kid. Seven-digit figures."

"What are you saying? Sometimes you go on and on. Do you remember that poker game where you and Andy started arguing about using the ace as a one in a five-card straight to the five and—"

"Jack! I think the seven-digit numbers are just coded local telephone numbers. Just some more time to check, until tomorrow, and I'll have all the numbers for you."

"Wow! Why didn't you say so? If you're right, I owe you a night on the town. Good work."

"Hey, Jack, what are you going to do, call the numbers and see who answers?"

"No, I've got a reverse phone book at the office that lists the phone number, and then the owner of the number and his address, just the opposite of what the Phone Company gives you. Only, I guess I can't go to my office right now. But I'll figure something out. I'll call you, and you can give me the numbers over the phone when I'm next to a reverse directory. Thanks. I hope you're right."

Awake two hours, and making progress already. If I could just see the opportunity in each difficulty, and not the difficulty in each opportunity, maybe the road to success wouldn't always be under repair. I just hoped time wasn't running out on me.

I couldn't go to my office to get my reverse phone book. I know there were probably agents from both camps eyeballing the one place I was supposed to be. Maybe I could get to the library and use the reverse listings on the Internet. I was convinced the secrets of the book would solve the legal dilemma I was in. I knew the Fat Man was hot for its return—maybe hot enough to kill for it. As long as I knew where the book was and he didn't, I wouldn't be killed. But I might be "persuaded" to talk, and I'd always had a strong aversion to torture, avoiding it wherever possible.

I wanted to put things into perspective and get a handle on this situation. Things had run along out of control for too long. I was going to take charge, get in the driver's seat, be captain of my ship, the Top Cat, Numero Uno.

But the day was young, and I hadn't read the paper yet or called the dreaded answering machine. Before I did that, I'd need a second cup of coffee. Can't do that in jail. No sir. You didn't get a second cup in jail. I flipped on the radio.

I was standing in front of Cooper's refrigerator, trying to decide whether to use milk or vanilla ice cream in my coffee, when I heard the radio crackle with a cold slap of reality. The newscaster was reading, "...and State and local police today are continuing their search for a Boston private investigator wanted for questioning in the serial killings on the Boston waterfront."

I spilled coffee down the front of my pants.

Then I heard the voice of State Police Detective Sergeant Jeffrey Houston.

"We are well-acquainted with Jack Kelly, and there is no arrest warrant for the former police detective at this time. We expect him to surface soon. You ask if he is a suspect? Not at this time. Kelly was the last to see some of the victims alive, and we have established certain links. We just want to question him further."

I'm on the News! My mother would roll over in her grave.

The newscaster went on to speak of the victims, with the addition of the midget, Benny Lopes, found in a cardboard box at my

Chinatown detective agency. The ME's office had ruled the snapped neck of the small man fit the MO of the serial killer.

The mood of my day had changed as quickly as the New England weather. A traveling sideshow passes through my office and suddenly I'm knee deep in quicksand, sucking me closer to a life in prison.

The State Police would most likely take the investigation up a notch and move it into a higher gear with their nationwide data base and psychological profilers. They could get court-ordered wiretaps on any phone number they thought I might call. That meant no more calls to the girlfriend. I knew I shouldn't even call my office. They probably had some kind of caller identification gizmo that would tell them what number I was calling from. I'd have to call from a pay phone. It was hard to imagine they would anticipate me calling my accountant, but next time, I'd call him from a pay phone, too.

I was thinking like a criminal again, but maybe I needed to. Even though I was innocent, I needed to think like a criminal. It was a matter of survival. Maybe that was the rush criminals thrived on. The struggle for survival…in a desperate situation…Being hunted.

I'd done plenty of undercover work in my years and I found an old paint-spattered jump suit of Cooper's and put it on. With a stocking cap on my head and a pocket full of change, I headed out onto the street and to the nearest pay phone. Then I decided I better go to a pay phone a bit farther away, devious criminal that I am. I called the machine.

Beep. Click.

Beep. Click.

Beep. "Detective Sergeant Jeff Houston, Mass State Police. Get in touch with me as soon as possible, John. A matter most important."

Beep. "Jack Kelly? Your Walther has been fit with night sights, whenever you want to pick it up." The gunsmith at the local police supply store said.

Beep. Click.

Beep. Click.

Beep. "Jack, its Joe. Call me. I think I've got good news." I hear the Bean Counter again. I've already talked to him. I hoped they hadn't traced his call.

Beep. Click.

Beep. "I've got to talk to you, I'll call back," said a female voice.

It sounded eerily like Bella Pavoni and the hairs stood up on the back of my neck. But I'd seen Bella staring back at me from the floor of the abandoned rail car on Pier 4 with a broken neck. I saw them photographing her cold corpse from every angle until it was time to ship her in a body bag to the morgue. There the paper bags would be taken off of her hands and her fingernails scraped and checked for evidence, just before they thoroughly probed every orifice and internal organ, dissected the contents of her stomach, taken blood samples, tissue samples, vitreous fluid from her eyeballs, and a sample of brain matter. They would know her physically quite well by the end of their inquiry.

The dreaded answering machine had done me in, again.

The Bean Counter must have called earlier, before I had spoken to him. But that female voice must've been someone in need of detective services. I didn't know why it sounded like Bella to me—I hadn't gotten the chance to hear much from Bella the night I'd met her.

Maybe I just wanted to hear a female voice. Ever since I'd left my girlfriend at the Bostonian, not knowing when I would see her again, I'd needed to hear a compassionate, reassuring voice. I was just reading the other day in a magazine, that women are controlled by the sensitive, nurturing, caring part of the brain...and men are controlled by the penis part of the brain.

Well, it wasn't The New England Journal of Medicine I was reading, I think it was PlayBoy. This was the same article that said men don't suffer from premature ejaculation...women do. The article stated that it takes a woman twenty-five minutes of exercise just to get breathing heavy and it takes a man just two minutes to get breathing heavy, just by watching her.

I had to get over to my office and get my reverse phone book. I'd order some Chinese food to be delivered here at Coop's, wait until dark, and slip over there. In and out. I'd be a shadow. A silent knight. An invisible ninja.

My office building was on the edge of Chinatown, overlooking the Southeast Expressway and the Central Artery. There were Asian restaurants on every street and corner. As a steady rain began to fall and thunder rolled in the distance, I slipped down the alleyway behind my building and walked towards the fire escape that went up to my office window on the fourth floor. The dark alley was thick with the aroma of chicken and pork fried rice. The few kitchen workers I could see down the block were too busy unloading a poultry truck to notice me as I skipped over puddles and avoided the rapid rivers forming in the gutters of the alleyway.

The heavy rain kept a steady beat, rapping and tapping out its syncopated rhythms on the hoods, roofs, and trunks of parked cars. Taps, raps, thuds, knocks, dings, dongs, booms, and splashes. The beat was infectious.

I disrespectfully stepped on the hood of an old junk Ford, fortuitously parked under the fire escape. Up I went, like smoke. I made no sound, a cat like ninja. Soon I was looking down on the street scene. There was no sign of a stakeout. They'd have to be as crazy as I was to be out in this driving thunderstorm.

I stood outside the fogged-up window of the bathroom and slid the window lock over with my driver's license. My own office security had never been a big thing with me. There wasn't anything there to steal that wasn't locked in the wall safe.

I opened the fogged-up bathroom window and slid in out of the rain, feet first. I got down by the john, lifted the lid, and was in the process of draining the lizard when I thought I heard voices in the outer office. I stopped in midstream, and looked out through the partially open door.

There were three men standing around in my outer office, talking and laughing. I became wide eyed with fear, adrenaline rushing through me.

My office had been ransacked. The front office door was split wide open, and had been kicked in. They didn't look like cops. I had to get out of there, fast.

I started to back up and out, onto the windowsill, but I leaned on the handle and the toilet flushed. Some shadow. Some silent ninja.

I prayed they hadn't heard. I peered out of the slightly ajar door. They looked in my direction, then continued talking, briefly.

It took three strides for the taller, skinny one of the three to get to the bathroom door. He reached inside the bathroom, grabbed me by the front of my jacket, and pulled me out, throwing me up against the office wall.

"Who are you?" he demanded.

Before I could invent some preposterous tale of who I was, and why I happened to be stopping in to use this particular bathroom, the biggest of the three stepped forward. "It's the comedian!"

"Hi, Bob," I said in a weakened voice. "How's little Bob?"

His face looked like a road map, with scar tissue and pockmarks. I imagined a few fights and years of heavy drinking had helped carve the terrain.

"Your mouth's been writin' checks your body can't cash, boy, but you can't walk it like you talk it!" Bob said.

I was impressed with his attempt at poetry. He had a tattoo on his right biceps that said "Born To Die." The man was not the sharpest knife in the draw. I don't think he could pour water out of a boot with instructions on the heel. Too much yardage between the goal posts.

Bob clenched his jaw. I wished I hadn't gone for the wise remark—it was a reflex. He hit me with a sucker punch; a right cross that hit me just below the left eye. I saw stars and little silver lights swimming around as my knees buckled. My eyes rolled upward, and I saw the electrical circuit breaker panel on the wall above me. I put my hands up in a position of surrender, my right hand just a few inches away from the two master switches.

"Hey, Ray, why's he call you Bob?" the skinny guy said. "You know him? Your name's not Bob. Is it? I got a...what do you call it...a pornographic memory, and I never heard you called Bob. Momma calls you Ray. Hey, Billy. Have you ever heard Momma call Ray Bob?"

Ray-Bob slapped Skinny across the face.

"This is the "defective" who's got the book, and be careful what you say! You told him my name! Are you gonna give him our address, too? Get that poker by the fireplace, Jack Kelly's gonna do the talking now...aren't ya, Jack? Or we're gonna start by breaking your toes. Then the bones in your feet, legs, then your fingers and hands. Any questions, Kelly?"

"Yes. If the grass is always greener on the other side, does it still need mowing? And what makes the sky blue, Bob? Can vegetarians eat animal crackers? What was the best thing before sliced bread?

And just how much wood can a woodchuck chuck, if a woodchuck really can chuck wood? Bob. Er, Ray…Ray-Bob?"

"See if he's packin' Billy!" Ray-Bob ordered.

As Skinny reached for the fireplace poker one of them fell over, crashing to the floor and drawing the attention, for a split second, of Ray-Bob, and Billy. This was my chance, probably my last.

I pulled down the master circuit breakers next to my hand, and all the lights went out. I took one step in the darkness toward the door and slammed Billy into Ray-Bob with a side thrust kick that knocked them both into the wall and onto the floor. Skinny bumped into something. "My leg!" he yelled in pain.

I knew the layout of my office in the dark—I had stumbled out of there in darkness for years. I could hear the three thugs struggling to get up, and moving in the right direction.

Ray-Bob was barking orders. "Get him! Don't let him leave!"

I was the first to get to the doorway. I turned and looked back into the darkness. A flash of lightning came through the windows. In that flash, I saw Ray-Bob and he saw me. He was moving toward me, smiling insanely, with a look of both rage and frustration on his face.

And with a knife in his hand.

CHAPTER 19

Dead Right

Moments like that help you to appreciate life and all its glory, the strife and challenge that we all overcome. The mountains we climb. The long road we travel, with much laughter, and many tears. The things we do, and the things we never got to. The end could come so fast.

I'd been thinking about death, even more than usual. Ever since I'd seen Bella staring in my direction, I'd been wondering how someone snaps a neck. Did you turn it a certain way? Did it make a cracking sound? Did the victim die instantly, or were they paralyzed for a bit?

I didn't want to die, but I knew no one gets out of here alive. We're all going to die. Little, sweet children, loving mothers, hard working fathers, the good, the bad, the beautiful. Gentle, silver haired grand folks.

I certainly didn't want to be murdered. Killed, chilled, whacked, rubbed out, knocked off, clipped, snuffed, popped, or hit. Put to sleep. I didn't want to buy the farm or sleep with the fishes.

But, maybe the Big One wasn't as bad as it's been cracked up to be? Transmigration of the soul to another plain. We move up or down the evolutionary food chain depending on whether we learned anything in this life. Maybe one faded into death—no pain, no strain, no fear or anxiety. Just a slip into the quiet and peaceful. Dissolving into the big sleep. Maybe death wasn't so bad.

Death, where is thy sting? And we live in constant fear of it.

I thought I heard Ray-Bob run into the inner office door that I had managed to swing shut behind me. The hallway was dimly lit as I sprinted down the stairs. Visions of the assaults that were about to be committed on me propelled me down the four flights of stairs and out into the heavy rain on the street. If the cops had the place staked out, this would be a good time for them to step out and make themselves known.

I ran full tilt over the wet streets and out of Chinatown, through the Financial District, and past the Boston Aquarium. I jogged through the Haymarket, speed-walked across the bottom of Beacon Hill, walked through the Boston Common, and filtered into the Combat Zone.

I was glad I'd stayed in shape, even though I had an occasional cigar or beer. I swam, windsurfed, played basketball regularly, and had been taking karate all these years. But I much preferred flight to fight.

I knew I could have pulled my .45 and emptied the clip into those goons, but what a mess they would have made, quarts of blood all over the office floor. It's an old building and the blood probably would have run through the cracks in the floor down onto the canvasses in the art studio below. After the canvasses dried, perhaps there could have been a showing, revealing the newest style of paintings, done with blood on canvass. The blood dripping on, and splashing across, the canvasses, the lines and circles were creating the true spirit of modern urban life. So very cool...So very cold.

CHAPTER 20

Zen Detective in the Combat Zone

If the cops had my office under surveillance, those three goons couldn't have kicked in my office door, turned the lights on, and ransacked the place. If the cops didn't have my office eyeballed, I doubted they had the Naked i under surveillance. I knew Ray-Bob caught up with me at the office, but this was a public place, and I had the book. They wouldn't gun me down in a strip club in the middle of the Combat Zone. Would they? It was getting to the point where I thought that maybe I should be in police custody, for my own protection.

I went into the Naked i. I needed to talk to an old friend, and bartender Ed McGee fit the profile. We hadn't exactly walked through hell together, but we'd gone through some wild and offbeat experiences on the road as we chased the rock and roll dream. We'd worked real hard for a long time, but there'd been nothing else we'd rather have been doing. Ed always seemed to put things into perspective for me.

I walked in and sat at the darker end of the bar, where Ed was at his usual station. There were only about a dozen businessmen from downtown sitting at the horseshoe bar. They were drinking, talking, and looking up as the strippers came out in an endless parade of glamour and seductiveness.

Ed brought me a shot of the good scotch. It was a tradition whenever I came in, Ed put out the scotch. It didn't matter if I drank it or not. Ed had quit drinking seven years before and I saluted him.

"I think I'll put this to good use today, Ed. Slide me a bottle of beer, too."

Ed got the beer and leaned over close.

"Man you're hot, Jack! Your picture is in the evening Boston Globe."

I almost spit the beer across the bar. "What page?"

"What page? Jesus, man. Aren't you concerned for yourself? Those hoods have been in here a few times hangin' around. They're looking for you, Jack! And a couple of State Police detectives, with their clean faces, short hair, and suits, were in here last night."

"I just interrupted some goons ransacking my office, and what they were going to do to me, well, it wasn't pretty, Ed. I just ran down here to see an old friend." I was getting heavy with Ed, but I knew he could take it.

"Okay, Jack. What can I do to help?"

"What page?" I repeated.

Ed gave the friendly look of resignation that came from knowing me for a long time. "The front page of the Metro Section."

"The front page of The Metro. Good picture?"

"The picture from before you were with the Burglary Task Force, or the Cold Case Squad. You were still a patrolman. They're talking about you on the radio, too. On a talk show this morning they were debating whether you're the serial killer or not!"

"In uniform, oh Jesus. I never liked the photos in uniform. Couldn't they find a shot of me in plain clothes? I wonder if my father still gets the Globe. He doesn't listen to talk radio."

Ed was shaking his head. Somehow, I had gotten what I'd come for.

"All right, Ed. I'm going. If I can, I'll try to meet you at The Rat, tomorrow at two o'clock. See if you can find out anything about Reno or the serial killer's victims, okay? Watch your back. Okay?"

The Rat was a little rock and roll club in Kenmore Square, between Fenway Park and Boston University, right downstairs from where Ed lived. It was originally named the Rathskeller but when it went to a rock and roll format, the name got shortened to The Rat. At night, it was rock and roll, but it was real quiet during the afternoon.

I walked out to the back bar at The Naked i with my hat down over my eyes. I slipped out the back door and into a cab at the stand on the corner.

After making sure I wasn't being followed, I had the cab drop me a couple of blocks from South Station, a couple blocks from Cooper's loft. It was getting late, and things didn't seem to be going my way.

It had stopped raining, and the moon was visible through passing clouds. The walk in the fresh air was the best thing that had happened to me that day. It was a quiet walk, on a dark street—and a chance to reflect. I wasn't digging my way out, I was getting buried.

I couldn't just turn myself over to the cops. That would tie me up, it would tie them up, and I didn't have anything to give them. I didn't know who was snapping necks. I didn't know why. I wasn't sure I cared. All I had was a gut feeling, a half-baked theory, and a couple of loose ends.

Bella, the Fat Man, and the midget visited my office. Bella and the midget are dead.

Bella had the book, the Big Round One wanted the book. Bella is dead.

I had the book. The Big Round One wanted the book…

I needed a vacation, somewhere by a beach. For me, stress dissolved in salt water. A place with warm gentle winds. Maybe I'd do some windsurfing, some scuba diving, a little golf, and plenty of fishing. Some good food and maybe even a little romance. No work. Just play…

I was going to need some money. This thing was preventing me from earning my living. I needed the cash, the bread, the dough, the bacon, the dead presidents, the green, the scratch. I had rent and taxes to pay. The only thing worse than paying income tax was not having an income to pay taxes on.

I got a Globe from a newspaper vending machine and headed for Cooper's fourth floor loft on South Street. All seemed quiet. I checked the street in front, and the alley in the back. There was hardly anybody on the back streets tonight.

I slipped into the building and up to the loft. After mixing a scotch and soda with a twist of lemon, I kicked back on the couch, turned the Celtics-Lakers game on the television with the sound off. I found a great oldies show, Little Walter's Time Machine on the radio. This guy played real chestnuts—the original rhythm and blues, and soul classics. Maybe I was trying to ease the pain.

My mind circled and then landed on the inevitable. Back to square one. What was it all about? All through majoring in philosophy in college and even now, that's what I asked myself. Today, and in this case, it seemed to be about power, control, fame, and lust. Those things were what drove us…and sometimes led us…to murder.

I didn't want to think about the spot I was in, but I wasn't fighting it when my mind inescapably wandered to certain aspects of the case. It was a trance-like state of mind, where the new age detective would do some creative thinking. Detachment. Like water, the mind would seek its own level. I was Zen Detective.

Tae Kwon Do taught there were equal opposites, yin and yang. Heaven and Earth. In and out. Up and down. Fire and Water. And so it was on this night, after a bad day, my dreams were peaceful and controlled.

CHAPTER 21

The First Time I Met The Blues

Johnny's Blues and Jazz Club was happening tonight. The atmosphere was just right. And the timing—there had been a buzz for days. It was the regular Blues Night at Johnny's, but on this night, appearing in my little club, was the Legend, all the way from Chicago, born in Mississippi, the Real Thing, the man who wrote the book on the blues—Mr. Muddy Waters. The Man Himself. Howlin' Wolf and John Lee Hooker on guitars, Willie Dixon on bass, Pine Top Perkins on piano, Paul Butterfield on blues harp, a three-piece horn section, and Keith Moon on drums.

That's right. Keith Moon on drums. It's my dream, and there's just no way of knowing who will show up. It was The All Dead Men

Band. Everybody is excited. I'm as proud as a peacock. This is the place to be. Who knows, maybe Jimi Hendrix will show up to jam. It could happen. In a dream.

The house is packed with trendsetters and the area's top musicians. Every top Boston band is represented by at least a few members. The beautiful people are here—actors, sports figures, agents, managers, writers, and those that always seem to be at every event. The door has sold out and people are still showing up just to stand outside and listen.

That glorious hum of cash registers and fluids being poured has brought a tear to my eye. To think that what was once an empty corner bar room, a vacant pit that smelled of stale beer and cigarettes, was now, simultaneously, the hottest and coolest spot in the Hub, the center of the universe. This is still the greatest country on earth.

The Blues Patrol, a group of local musicians consisting of me on guitar, and some of my friends, had done an excellent job of rendering solid, soulful, urban blues as the opening act. The level was building. Excitement, as they say, was mounting. The All Dead Men Band would be going on soon.

I took my usual spot at the dark end of the bar. I had my bartender, James, get me a cognac tonight. I lit the Royal Jamaica cigar I'd been keeping in my jacket pocket all day. As the smoke curled upwards, the house lights dimmed. From the darkened stage, I could hear the musical instruments being tuned and blues riffs being checked. Then the deep, dark, and delicious voice of Mr. Muddy Waters said, "This is the blues."

The complete history of the blues was laid out by these masters in words and music. From the slave ships to the cotton fields, from the beginnings of life here in the land of the free, until freedom from slavery and tyranny was actually attained, if indeed it has been attained. From the sounds of the country life down south to the mechanized hammer of urban Chicago blues. Dealing with The Man, the basic relationships of men and women, the respect that a man needs, then more about the relationships between men and women. The long days of work and suffering. The pain and joy of the family. The mixed messages and the promise of America. This was the blues.

This made for a night to remember at Johnny's. At the end of the show, some people shook my hand as they were leaving. Maybe they were dreaming, too. After the band was gone and the club was cleared out, James and I had a drink together. We looked at each other and smiled.

James, Dinky the soundman, and the last waitress were leaving for the night, when the waitress popped her head back in the front door.

"Good night, Jack. Oh, the band's manager is out here, he wants to talk to you."

The front door closed. I had already paid the band. Maybe the manager wanted to thank me.

Then the door burst open, and there blocking the doorway stood the largest, fattest human being I had ever seen. His straining white eyes peered out intensely from the rolls of fat. Buttons burst from his shirt and he seemed to be growing even larger, inflating to the bursting point. The Fat Man shook as he screamed in his guttural voice, "You've got to pay. You've got to pay! You've got to pay more! You owe me something! You've got my something! Give me my book!"

Startled, I awoke to the bright sun.

CHAPTER 22

The Sister

It was another bright, cool, Boston day. The long hot Indian Summer was turning into deep fall. It was Monday, the beginning of the work week, a chance to set the record straight. A chance to put the world back on its axis, to make the world right again.

It wasn't like I was a fugitive. I hadn't any official notification that I was wanted. I could always say I was staying at Cooper's loft, hadn't seen the television, didn't listen to the radio, and hadn't bought the newspapers. I could have been reading Tolstoy's "War and Peace," Shakespeare's "Macbeth", Dante's "The Inferno", or perhaps "The Tibetan Book of the Dead" all weekend. Had I been warned, I mean notified, that I could be of some service to law enforcement agencies, being a concerned citizen, of course I would want to help.

The day's early objectives were as follows—check the news on television, the radio, and in the newspapers. Check the dreaded answering machine, if it was still plugged in. Speak with the Bean Counter, and regroup for lunch at the Rat with Ed McGee. My friend Sergeant Jim Watson should be back from his fishing trip, but I didn't think I should contact him. I didn't want him to ask me to come in.

I put on the paint-spattered coveralls, a painter's hat, and went out and picked up the Globe and Herald, some coffee, and a couple of cheap cigars at the local shop down the street. Before I returned to the loft, I hit the pay phone on the corner. I was feeling good. Like I could make a difference. I was a free man. I wasn't hurt. This mix-up, this misunderstanding, could clear up at any moment. It was a beautiful day.

But the happy glow soon wore off like the smell of cheap perfume and cigarette smoke as I listened to the dreaded answering machine.

"John, it would be in your best interest to contact me right away at State Police headquarters, 1010 Commonwealth Avenue. This is Detective Sergeant Jeff Houston."

Beep. Click. Beep. "Jack. Gordon Little from WBZ. Look, if it's a question of money, we can work something out for an exclusive. Tell your side of the story. Give a call."

Beep. "I'll see you at the established coordinates," said Andy, my poker buddy.

Beep. Click. Beep. "I've got to see you. My sister, she left your card on her bed. I don't know why, but you've got to help me. Please call. Maria Pavoni." She left her phone number.

It was the mysterious woman's voice I'd heard on the answering machine before. I scribbled down the number. Ever the optimist, I hoped this was a break and not a trap. Maybe she heard Bella had given me some money and wanted it back. Maybe there was no Maria Pavoni. But that voice—it had to have come from the same lineage as Bella. The hair on the back of my neck stood up as I heard her speak. I would investigate it later.

After dialing the Bean Counter's number and getting no answer, I returned to the loft, and winced with anticipation as I opened the Boston newspapers.

The Globe had only a recap on page two in the Metro section, with a small picture of me the size of a postage stamp in the corner of the article. It said "Private Investigator" under the photo. It didn't even mention my name. It didn't have anything new in it, but the article mentioned that police were seeking a Boston private investigator for questioning. The Herald had an article on page three, with a picture of Detective Sergeant Jeff Houston of the State Police, and Sergeant Bill Rogers of the BPD Homicide Unit. The article focused on the forming of a task force to coordinate the investigation into the serial killings.

The sound and the fury, signifying nothing. The Herald article was a brief recap, but no mention of me at all. I almost felt slighted. Was I yesterday's news? Maybe things were quieting down. Or maybe it was the calm before the storm.

CHAPTER 23

The Transvestite & The Hacker

In this business, some of the best information could be obtained in the quickest way by the use of the pretext phone call. It was basically coercing, cajoling, scamming, or somehow convincing someone to give you some information, usually by some slight deception or false pretense.

I was pretty good at it. Basically I was lazy, and I'd cut a corner and skip to the chase if I could. Why would I drive all the way to Worcester to see if a certain car was in the driveway of a certain residence, if I can call the old lady who lives across the street from that certain residence, and tell her some lie so she can look out her window and tell me if that certain car is parked at that certain

Johnny Barnes

residence? I could get the old lady in Worcester's phone number from the reverse phone book, which lists streets and the name of who lived at the street number and what the phone number was at that location. A well-planned and well-executed pretext phone call could save days of work and expense.

I settled in to do some phone work. There was no problem with using Cooper's phone, as I wasn't calling any numbers I suspected might be tapped or trapped. I started with directory information. Off the top of my head, I asked for the number for Digby Riggs. The operator said she had no listing. I asked her for Kim French, the name Digby used when he worked as a transvestite. No listing. Before she could hang up, I asked for a listing on Robert Black, the name on the entertainer's driver's license. She had seventeen Robert Blacks. I didn't know the street.

I know Mr. Black was dead, but figured somebody might live at his residence, maybe a girlfriend or wife who could tell me something. I was shooting in the dark. I wasn't ready to call Bella's sister Maria until I had some direct questions for her. I opened the Yellow Pages to the entertainment listing. There was one

150

entertainment-booking agency that offered exotic dancers, musicians, and special "Party Packages." I called and explained to the lady that I had repaired a Gibson Les Paul guitar for a Mr. Digby Riggs, and he hadn't picked it up. I asked if she knew his number, so I could have him pick it up.

The poor girl at the Diamond Talent Agency proceeded to tell me of the demise of Digby Riggs and what a sweet man he was. I asked if he had a loved one at home that would want his expensive and beloved guitar. No charge for the work done, of course. She told me she thought that he had a lady friend at home who sometimes helped him with his act. She gave me the number.

I called the number and a young woman answered. I was winging it. I told her how sorry I was, I used to play in a blues band with Digby, and had just heard what happened.

"Robert hated the blues," she said.

"Yeah, I know. He said that's why he was leaving the band. Oh, that guy would have walked through fire for a friend."

"When did you play with Robert? I've been with him for seven years. Who are you?"

"It was about eight years ago. Bill Williams. I played bass with him and that other guitar player there, ah…" I stammered, ready to hang up.

"Lefty Crawford?"

"Yup. Lefty, me, and Digby, we were like brothers. Look, if I called at a bad time, I'm sorry, I just can't believe—"

"No, it's okay, Bill. I…I've been on edge. I mean the way they found him, tied up to a runway light pole. I'm Suki Jones. We were gonna get married." She was sniffling, crying.

"Suki, why did it happen? Did he owe money or have any enemies?"

"No. The paper says some psycho-killer did it."

"So there was nothing unusual going on?"

"Robert was unusual…every day. But he was not going to get a sex-change operation like that Gordon Little on that television station said! He was every inch a man."

That was as good a testimony as any I'd ever heard.

"Ah…did he know any of the others who had been killed?" I stammered.

"No. Well, yes. Robert hung around the Channel, where his friend the manager was killed. With that weird crowd. He played there with his rock band as Digby Riggs, and worked in the back lounge as Kim French."

It was interesting, but I knew that much. Either Suki Jones didn't have the answers, or I didn't have the right questions. I asked her if it would be all right to call her back sometime, just to make sure she was doing all right. She said she'd like that.

Next I attempted to locate a number for Gerard Spring, the computer hack found in his car on A Street and Broadway in Southie. There were only three Gerard Springs listed in the Boston area, none in Southie. I dialed up the Gerard Spring on Commonwealth Place. A young woman answered and told me Gerard was out taking his pet Boa Constrictor to Angel Memorial Animal Hospital for a check up. Never mind. It was obviously the wrong man.

The next had a Brighton Avenue address, and there was no answer. I tried the third and final number listed, a number in Milton, a town on the southern outskirts of Boston. An older woman answered.

"Hi. Is Gerard Spring there?" Desperate times called for desperate measures.

"Who's calling?"

"McKinley Morganfield." I said, using Muddy Waters' real name.

"What is this in reference to?"

"I'm interested in hiring Mr. Spring to do some consulting. My restaurant business computers are in need of upgrading, or uploading, or...ah...I won't try to fool you—I don't know anything about the damn things."

"You know, I hate those damn things, too! I have trouble with the television remote control. But Gerard loved 'em, Mr...?"

"McKinley Morganfield. Call me Mac. Are you Mr. Spring's daughter?" This worked every time.

"No, I'm his mother. I was..." She choked up a little.

"I'm sorry. Is something wrong? Did something happen? I can call back."

"He's had an accident. And he was killed. The whole family misses him so much. He's got a little room in the garage where he started with the computers. Sometimes he wouldn't come out for days. I'd bring him food. Nice meat and potatoes. A little pie. He loved his Key Lime pie. He wouldn't stop to eat if I didn't bring it!"

I was beginning to realize Mrs. Spring might go on and on. I needed to steer her in the right direction.

"That's so hard on you. You poor soul."

"I can't bear to go into the garage and see that computer in the middle of his big desk. It's like a shrine!"

"Mrs. Spring, who was Gerard working for at the time of his—I'm sorry—car accident?"

"The serial killer. Can you believe it?"

"Who was he working for, Mrs. Spring?"

"He worked for a lot of different people and businesses. I don't know much about his work, unless he happened to mention it. He worked for a computer dating company. They get dates by the computer. Can you believe that? In my day, we picked a boy we were sweet on, you know, someone we had a crush on, and we'd sit and talk for hours. Maybe an ice cream soda, maybe hold hands or a long walk. We'd never—"

"Mrs. Spring."

"Oh, where was I? Gerard usually goes into a business, like yours, and sets up his programs, or whatever. He's worked for big and small. He was even working for Lieutenant Governor King on his election campaign. How did you come to call on Gerard, Mr. Mac?"

"Well, ah, I was having lunch with a few businessmen last week, and someone recommended him."

"Who was that?"

"Ah, that would have been…well, ah, you know, I think it was the bartender." I was wondering if she was going to buy that.

"That must have been at the Channel."

"Uh huh," I mumbled.

"He did their computers for next to nothing, just to socialize and meet the girls, my boy…"

She'd bought it.

I was a sensitive guy and she was sobbing a bit. I just didn't want to go on hoodwinking the sweet woman. I told her I was sorry to disturb her in her sorrow. I told her it was good to grieve for awhile, but to be kind to herself and not to punish herself, no one would want that.

CHAPTER 24

At The Rat

With sunglasses, my face unshaven, hat pulled down, collar up on my overcoat, I was hardly recognizable. I was ready for lunch upstairs at the Rat. The cab dropped me off in Kenmore Square, a couple of blocks from Fenway Park, and I was up the stairs and into the Rat to meet Ed McGee at a table in the back. Ed got up and let me sit with my back to the wall where I could see out the door.

We made a little small talk until a waitress dropped off a couple of sandwiches. Ed couldn't believe the predicament I was in. I couldn't, either. He asked me what my plans were. I told him I didn't think Jesus could save me.

I told him I planned to wake up the next day and all of it would be straightened out. Maybe Cinderella or the Tooth Fairy would sprinkle some magic dust and the whole thing would go away—some demented soul would be in custody, charged with reckless disposal of eight bodies. The maniac's picture would be splashed all over the media. I would fade into peaceful oblivion.

"Seriously, Jack. Why don't you get out of Dodge for a while, until they do find the killer? They won't charge you with any unlawful flight or anything after they catch the Snapper."

"Hey! The Snapper. I like that. Where'd you get that one? Did you just make that up?"

"No, I heard a couple of the girls call him The Snapper. A customer, too. The Neck Snapper."

"Do you think the Snapper has a copycat yet?" I asked.

"Amateurs copy, professionals steal," Ed said.

"Did you just make that up?"

"No. Somebody said that. Keith Richards, I think. Where are you staying?"

"You don't want to know. But I may have to go deeper underground if this keeps up. I'm apparently a suspect in these serial killings. It's disrupting my life. I don't know if I can go to my Regular Rotating Super Secret Monday Night Poker Game tonight."

"If you need to, you know you can stay on the couch upstairs, right?"

"Thanks, Ed. What have you found out?"

"Nothing much. We've been busy all weekend. But I do know just from talkin' to a couple of know-it-alls that come into the club that Reno may be thought of in some circles as a garbage truck driver, but in state politics, he's buying his way into the inner circles. He has contributed heavily to the arts, museums, civic programs, and any other cause that will take his money. Including Lieutenant Governor King's campaign for election to Governor."

"I guess that could possibly account for why the cops aren't breathing down Reno's neck. They must have at least questioned him. Bella was his girlfriend. The midget worked for him. He's got a stronger connection to them than I do. Why don't they put his picture in the goddamn newspaper?"

"Cool it, Jack. Geez."

I was yelling. "All right. Sorry, Ed. See if you can dig up some more on Reno, and I'll call you. Or I'll stop by the Naked i."

I had Ed flag me a cab from the stand in Kenmore Square. The Red Sox game had just gotten out from Fenway Park. The Sox had beaten the Yankees, and Kenmore Square was filled with happy baseball fans on their merry way home. I envied them.

As the cab ride took me down Boylston Street, we passed under the taller buildings in Boston. I had to find my way out of the woods. The cops weren't coming up with anything. So they formed a joint task force. Big deal. Somebody was snapping necks all over the waterfront, and they couldn't find him. But they could find a press conference with its photo opportunities. They could form a task force, all right. They thought I might know something, which I didn't, but they couldn't find me, either.

I got out of the cab at the Essex liquor store on the outskirts of the Combat Zone. I bought a six-pack of beer for the night's poker game, and walked through Chinatown to a pay phone a few blocks from Cooper's loft.

I dialed the number Maria Pavoni had left on my machine.

"Hello."

"Maria Pavoni?"

"Yes, this is."

"I got a message to call you. I'm—"

"I know who you are. You're the detective my sister contacted, aren't you? Oh, I'm so glad you called. I've been desperately hoping you could help me, Mr. Kelly."

"Just call me Jack, I don't like the 'Mr. Kelly,' it sounds like my father is in the room. And if my father is in the room, I'll have to watch my swearing, hide my cigar, and sit up straight. Now, how can I help you?"

"Bella told me she was going to see a private detective. I found your business card on her bed."

"Yeah, my card has been turning up a lot lately."

"Well, did you know what happened to her?"

"I know she was found in a rail car, with a snapped neck."

"Bella was the most upbeat, fun loving, bright, beautiful, artistic…" She began to sob.

"I didn't mean to bring up sad memories, Miss Pavoni."

"No, it's okay. I've got to talk to you. I've got to find out more about Bella's last few days. I feel I have parts of a puzzle, and I need more parts to put together a picture." I could relate to that. "Look. I understand. There are some questions I want to ask you, too. Let's meet tomorrow. I'll call this number in the morning with instructions on how, where, and when we'll meet."

She agreed, but sounded like she was as much in the dark as I was.

CHAPTER 25

The Regular Rotating Super Secret Monday

Night Poker Game

The secret was well guarded. It would take more than torture for the undisclosed location to be revealed. Privileged few were allowed into the inner circle, the inner sanctum. Decorum and general sensibility were tossed aside. Of course, I refer to the Regular Rotating Super Secret Monday Night Poker Game.

Only the charter members knew the location. No wives knew. No girlfriends knew. It was the equivalent of what we called the "He-Man Woman Haters No Girls Allowed Club" when we were kids. We were older now, and instead of trading baseball cards, we played poker and traded pictures of dead presidents. Exotic foods, drinks, and even women were ordered and delivered on rare occasion. Only certain "loose" females that were summoned showed up late in the night.

But it was a poker game. That was the main business. Nothing high stakes. A $2 maximum raise on the bets and a $5 limit. But the pots would hit $100 as the night progressed. The end result would be that one guy would be up a bit one week, and another guy would be up the next. It was just an excuse to get together and drink, smoke, gamble, and more not than often, womanize.

This week's game was at Fran's apartment in the Roxbury section of Boston. The apartment was on Massachusetts Avenue near Symphony Hall, where very late at night, the area is frequented by robbers, drug addicts, hookers, and trouble around every corner. It was a rough section. Most of us attending the game would leave in pairs or sometimes play poker all night and leave after breakfast when the sun came up.

Coop had arrived home late in the afternoon. At about nine, we rode over to the poker game in his Jeep. He told me about the models he'd shot over the weekend, I told him about the red reefer I had found on his coffee table and the nightmare about the Red Army Ants. We were still laughing as we pulled up in front of the Roxy, a bar near Fran's apartment.

What looked like three very attractive ladies of the evening approached us from the darkness at the corner as we got out of the car. They were definitely sending us signals. The closer they got, the more I realized the front two were beat. They had been around the block more than a few times. When they got closer, I realized painted lips and a blonde wig did not a beauty make.

The third streetwalker looked very young to be soliciting sex. I asked her how old she was, and she said twenty-one.

"No, really, girl?"

"Sixteen," she confessed.

"I was twenty-two when I was your age."

One of the older hookers spoke up. "Lookin' for a party? Want to have a good time? Get ya pipes cleaned? Ya hear what I'm sayin', pretty boys? You not cops, right? You gotta tell us if you cops, right?"

"Miss!" I said, pointing to Cooper. "This man is Reverend Heathcliff of the Saint Mary Catherine Margaret Church of the Blessed Bleeding Virgin, and he is here to administer the last rights to a dying lady in the apartment upstairs. And as that dear departing lady is my inbred sister, I'll ask you to take your `pipe cleaning' services back around the corner, if you would."

Like vampires who had been shown a cross, the ladies of the evening slipped back into the night.

Upon arrival at Fran's second-floor apartment, all the usual suspects were there—Fran, Andy, Ira, Kim. They were making change, unwrapping a new deck of cards, and settling down with libations at hand when we arrived. The tunes weren't rolling yet. That was my job.

One of the unofficial rules of the poker game was a sporting event had to be on television. This Monday there was a football game—the Miami Dolphins versus the New York Giants. It was the start of the regular season. I immediately bet $10 with Wiley, on the Giants, even though I liked Miami better. Miami was favored by three points according to the Las Vegas line. The game was in Miami but the Giants are tough and NFC teams match up well against AFC teams.

I found some classic Frank Sinatra and B.B. King to feed the stereo. The game was on television, the cards were flowing, the deal was rotating, and money was changing hands. Idle talk of sports, women, business, more sports and more women, abounded. Here I could chomp on a big cigar without offending anyone. I could sip expensive cognac and swill it down with cheap beer, without being accused of poor taste. There was nothing to prove and no one to impress.

It was a needed moment of respite from a bitter and distasteful reality. The monotony of the slow spiral down toward my demise was imperceptibly crushing my spirits.

Unlucky at cards, lucky in love. If it wasn't for bad luck, I wouldn't have no luck at all. I won some and lost some during the evening, but stayed about even. The Giants pulled through for me and beat Miami by a touchdown, putting me over the top for the night.

As all of the poker players except Fran, Coop, and myself left for the night, I noted the guys hadn't asked me any questions about being wanted as a suspect for questioning in the serial killings. Fran set me straight.

"Jack, anybody that knows you knows that you couldn't do anything like that. Not for a minute, man. You're an A-number-one stand-up guy, and we know it. We've known you for too many years to give a flyin' hoot about what anybody says." He paused for a moment, then added, "So, did you kill them people or what?"

I looked up, shocked. My old friend was pointing at me and smiling. "Gotcha!"

CHAPTER 26

The Moving Surveillance

I ended up staying at Fran's apartment in Roxbury. I didn't want to bring any more heat on Cooper, and I had stayed at his loft for a couple of days. Why not spread the heat around?

I've got an old, white, nondescript Ford Crown Victoria. It was my patrol car at one time, bought it at an auction. I call it Mighty Whitey. I keep it in a garage downtown for work mostly and basic transportation. For surveillance I usually rent, or borrow, something else. Kids, street people, and criminals can spot a cop car, or a former cop car, a mile away. But I didn't want to go near it. It would be just like the cops to locate my vehicle and sit on it. They might be doing some spot surveillance or an occasional drive-by.

What I had in mind was a little surveillance myself. Fran had an old, blue Chevy van with tinted windows, perfect for that kind of work. He said I could use it.

Moving surveillance, especially trying to follow a vehicle in the greater Boston area with all its little neighborhoods, was hard. The stop signs, traffic lights, the narrow streets, and one ways all make it difficult to keep the tail. You could lose the subject quickly. It was best to use at least two vehicles with radio communication between them. But that was in a perfect world. I was alone today.

I didn't have much of a plan. Each target location warranted a different method of operation. I picked up Fran's old blue van and headed for Big Boy's condo on Admiral's Hill in Chelsea to do a drive-by. I could see the doors and windows at 80 Captains Row were closed as I drove past the town houses.

It was a Tuesday morning, about 10 a.m., and Mr. King-size was probably away from home and working, but it felt good to be on the offensive. I didn't want to be pushed around any longer. I'm a detective.

I wished I had gone to the Department of Motor Vehicles and gotten a list of all the vehicles privately owned by Thaddeus Reno, but I didn't want to be spotted by any of the many cops that go in and out of the DMV. If I knew Reno's car was parked by his condo, maybe he was there, too.

I didn't know if he was home. This seemed like a good time for a pretext phone call to the Reno residence. I proceeded to a variety store down the hill and used the pay phone outside. The information operator told me Thaddeus Reno had an unlisted number, but I did get her to verify he lived at 80 Captains Row.

I picked up a sandwich, a cup of coffee, and the Boston papers and headed back to Reno's street. I found a parking space halfway down the block and parked the van facing away from Reno's. People didn't catch on too easily that they were being watched when the surveillance vehicle was facing another direction.

I found an old Red Sox cap in the back of the van and put it on. I punched the frequency of the Chelsea Police into the scanner Fran had left me. One word from the police dispatcher to a patrol unit about a suspicious vehicle in Reno's neighborhood, and I was gone. Out of business. I wouldn't be around when the patrol car arrived. I tuned the van's AM-FM radio into a call-in talk show. Today's topic was about teenage prostitutes and the men and women who use them.

I locked the doors from the inside and settled back in the overstuffed living room chair Fran kept in the back of the van. It could be a long day, but I would at least be comfortable. Not that I had anything more important to do, anyway. I had a full view of Reno's residence out of the right side window. Out of the left side, I could see past the Mystic Tobin Bridge, the Bunker Hill Monument, to Boston Harbor and Logan Airport.

Yes, crime was my business, and business was good. Except that if I couldn't resolve this case, I was going to be out of business. I couldn't remember how often I'd watched a building for many hours, and it hadn't moved once. That seemed to be the case today. Zero movement at the Reno residence.

I used my time wisely. I had read the papers—there was nothing new. I listened to police radio traffic involving an armed bank robbery and the foot chase that ended with the apprehension of the perpetrators. I wondered why the cops couldn't make an arrest in the

Snapper case. I pondered my situation. I had thought about what questions I could ask Maria Pavoni. I ate my lunch. And I had found out more than I ever wanted to know about teenage prostitutes and the men and women who use them.

By 3 p.m., I was about ready to pack it in for the day. I watched a wino, quite out of place for that neighborhood, stumble and stagger his way up the sidewalk, pausing only briefly to urinate on the van's rear tire. I took it as a sign from God.

As I slid up into the driver's seat preparing to leave, a big black Cadillac passed me and pulled up in front of Reno's condo. The Huge One oozed out from the front door of his apartment, his tiny bird feet looking as if they ached as he waddled down the front porch stairs and around to the passenger side of the two door Caddy. The car squeaked, groaned, and sank about six inches as Reno dropped onto the front seat. I don't think he could have fit in the back. He'd require a stretch limo for that.

We were on the move. In the last thirty seconds, I had gone from a state of boredom to a heightened, adrenaline-pumping chase mode. I had to keep up with Reno, but not let him or his driver notice I was following them. I didn't want this to be a case of the hunter being captured by the hunted. They could manipulate me down the wrong street and, well, the old van couldn't outrun a bicycle.

We left Chelsea, cutting through the produce center, and headed east on Route 16, the Revere Beach Parkway. I noticed the Cadillac's vanity plate, T-R-A-S-H. That would be registered to Reno Waste Management, no doubt.

The Caddy pulled over at a storefront on the side of the Parkway, Richie's Slush. I proceeded on for about half a block and pulled into a used car lot. Reno's driver went over to Richie's outside counter. He returned to the Caddy and handed over a small brown paper bag and a quart-sized red slush to the Fat Man.

There was something familiar looking about the driver. He was limping slightly, was tall and very, very thin. It was Skinny, one of the three thugs who had ransacked my office. The dark suit and chauffeur hat had thrown me off.

As the black Cadillac proceeded onward, I swung the van in behind a few cars back. We ended up cruising along Revere Beach, the island of Nahant visible across the blue waters, under a clear blue sky. The Caddy stopped across from Kelly's Roast Beef. Skinny exited the vehicle, crossed the street, and went into the back door of Kelly's. He returned shortly with another small paper bag, three or four boxes of fried clams, three or four lobster rolls, and a bucket of fries. I felt like I was following the food critic for the Boston Globe.

The Big One completed his feeding frenzy, and the Caddy headed back towards Boston, my van two or three cars behind. I could see Reno speaking on a mobile phone while Skinny handled the driving. If only I could find the frequency his phone was using, I could set my scanner on it. I wanted to hear what he was saying. As I drove, I set the hand-held unit to scan the frequency range for mobile phones.

We passed the Wonderland dog track, and the Cadillac pulled into the Dunkin' Donuts at Bell Circle. Skinny picked up another small paper bag, a box of doughnuts, and delivered a giant Styrofoam cup of steaming Java to Reno. Then they proceeded on, by Logan International Airport and into Boston through the Callahan Tunnel, that nightmarish jungle of a traffic jam. That deep, black hole, where sunlight can't enter or escape, where you travel through the harsh glare of neon tubes and tiles that crossed beneath Boston Harbor into the city.

The scanner crackled. Scanning the appropriate frequencies had picked up one side of a mobile phone conversation. It was the transmission of some guy apparently talking to his wife. I could only pick up his side of the conversation. He was telling her he was just leaving the office, did she pick up the lobsters, and he would give the baby sitter a ride home. He seemed quite insistent on that.

The Cadillac exited the tunnel and took a sharp turn into the Haymarket section of Boston. I almost missed the turn, and hoped Skinny didn't notice me waving off cars as I tried to keep up. They pulled up next to a hydrant on the right, and I took a left and double-parked halfway down the street.

Reno climbed out of the car, and I followed both Fat and Skinny into Faneuil Hall Marketplace. I wondered what Reno might want in there—there was nothing but small food stands in Faneuil Hall. I'd answered my own question. Reno began sampling stuffed mushroom caps, sausages, knockwurst, pizza, oysters on the half-shell, shrimp, gelato, fruit cups, yogurt, cappuccino. I couldn't believe it.

After a lengthy visit to the public men's room, Reno began his duck-like waddle back towards the Caddy, Skinny at his side and I a distance behind. I had no trouble getting back to the van, turning it around, and preparing to follow while Reno got his big butt into his car.

The Cadillac turned back around the Boston Garden and headed west down Storrow Drive. I was beginning to sweat. I couldn't keep following this guy without being made. Some people, especially women, just never looked back. They only looked in the rear view mirror to check their hair and see if they looked all right. But these guys were going to realize there had been a ratty old blue van in the picture, everywhere they'd been today. It was only on television where the hero follows right behind the bad guys and they don't notice a thing. As I worried about what might happen if they confronted me, the scanner crackled and beeped.

A harmonized, oscillating, distorted voice came over the radio frequency. I became increasingly convinced it was the voice of Thaddeus Reno calling from the car ahead of me, as I could see his left hand up to his ear and see his head bobbing in time to the staccato sounds fading in and out over the scanner.

From the bits and pieces I could hear of the conversation, Reno was telling someone to be ready to be picked up. I could only hear Reno's side of the conversation, but he seemed very happy about something he was hearing.

"Good! Good! That item is important to me...handsomely rewarded."

I remembered how difficult it was to understand Reno in person. His deep, garbled voice made him sound as if he gargled with razor blades. The last thing I heard him say over the scanner as we headed by Mass General and through the Charles Circle Tunnel was about the book, and a handsome reward.

I set the scanner to stay on that frequency. If it became an extended surveillance, I could get directional microphones that could pick up conversations from fifty feet away and would record directly onto a micro-cassette recorder. But this would be no extended surveillance. I knew the case wasn't going to last that long.

Was the Round One talking about the same book that could be a key to this mystery? The book he wanted so badly? The book I've got? Was it the book Mr. Big may have killed for and may be keeping me alive?

CHAPTER 27

Shake, Rattle, and Roll

The Cadillac pulled off of Storrow Drive and onto Beacon Street. I stayed back and stopped two blocks away when the Caddy crossed Mass. Ave. and pulled up in front of The Crossroads bar and restaurant. The thin man held the doors open, and it took a while, but Fatman managed to waddle into the restaurant.

Was this guy going to eat again? Have mercy! Someone should've called the Bureau of Weights and Measures. Maybe the rescue unit or the bomb squad. He could explode at any minute.

I didn't expect Reno to come skipping right back out and hop in the car. He didn't move quickly. I was getting a little hungry myself, having built up an appetite watching him eat. I drove quickly one block over to Marlborough Street and pulled up to Mass. Ave., where I could see the back half of the black Caddy around the corner. I got out and crossed the street to a small variety store. I got a miniature blueberry pie in a box and a pint of milk—not quite the cuisine I'd observed the Human Vacuum suck down, but then again I didn't weigh nearly seven-hundred pounds, and I could look down and see my feet.

I could just see the big tail fin of the Caddy from the pay phone in front of the store. I called Joe Panetta, the Bean Counter. He told me he had taken his investigation into the book about as far as it would go. He said there were two sets of books, definitely for the same business. Joe said the two lists of numbers in the back were telephone numbers probably connected to the businesses involved. He suspected that one list was legitimate and the other list were businesses that participated in some kind of crooked scheme resulting in the altered account.

I told him I would pick up the book later that night and we'd talk at length then. I had to find a safe place to keep it. Bad luck and trouble seemed to follow that book. Maybe it was time to get it to Sergeant Jim Watson for safekeeping. I'd turn it over that night.

The Cadillac was still parked, so I called Maria Pavoni. I listened closely to the tone of her voice, focusing on any slight nuance that might tip me off as to what she may know, think, or expect. She was still a mystery. She sounded sincere in her desire to find out just what had happened to her sister.

I asked her what she knew about it, and she said nothing other than what the police had told her about finding Bella's body in the rail car. I asked her if she knew Thaddeus Reno, and she stated she knew him well enough to know he disgusted her with his personal habits and the way he treated her sister like his possession. She had only met him two or three times, once backstage at a play that featured Bella in a starring role. Reno had financially backed the play. She was impressed with Reno, patron of the arts, at first. Shortly after, Reno bought Bella the big pink Cadillac and they became a couple.

The second time she'd met Reno was in the hospital when she visited Bella, who supposedly had taken a fall resulting in some nasty bruises and contusions on her face. Reno didn't leave Bella alone with anyone, staying by her side for two days. Maria speculated it might have been because Reno didn't want Bella telling anyone how she really got those bruises.

Maria sounded level-headed to me, and I liked that. She thought Reno was disgusting, so her sensibilities were intact. There was enough weirdness going on around town to last me the rest of the year. I wanted normal.

My eyes almost popped out of my head as Skinny suddenly turned the corner and briskly walked towards me. I turned my back and watched him in the reflection on the phone booth glass as he entered the store and asked for a pack of cigarettes.

"Look, I have to go, Maria, I'm right in the middle of something."

"But Jack, you haven't told me anything about what you were working on for Bella!"

"I'll have to get back to you on that, uh, later tonight. I want to talk to you some more, Maria, okay?"

She asked me to call anytime, day or night. I told her I would as I watched Skinny exit the store and walk back towards the Cadillac.

I crossed the street and hopped in the van. I doubled back and resumed my former position on Beacon, with a full view of the Cadillac and the Crossroads. I wondered if the Big Man had eaten another meal. Skinny was leaning on the car smoking his third consecutive cigarette when Reno finally came out of the restaurant, accompanied by another man.

It was "Bob," my old friend from the Naked i, the leader of the pack that trashed my office. I wasn't happy to see him. He was not a nice man.

The three got into the car and drove on, and I was tagging right along. It was getting darker. Soon it would be a little easier to follow them without being noticed. But now there were three sets of eyes to worry about.

I followed the big black Cadillac onto Storrow Drive along the Charles River back towards downtown Boston. I set the scanner and put the Fat One's frequency on priority. The scanner picked up another one-sided conversation—it was a male calling and asking directions to an office building in Government Center so he could drop off some legal documents. As I attempted to pass a gray Chevy,

I saw the man in question, phone held tightly to his ear. I felt an urge to shout to him, "Get off at the Charles Street Jail and go up four blocks!"

The man in the gray Chevy accelerated and went right past his exit, quite lost, but the Caddy took a right at Charles Street and I followed. I could hardly believe it when Reno's ride went right past Buzzy's Roast Beef without turning in for a quick snack.

I was getting more tense about following Reno in the downtown area when they took a right and started heading up the side streets of Beacon Hill. Rows of red brick townhouses lined the winding streets. This was worse. On the narrow, one-way, twisting, labyrinthine, cobblestone streets that covered Beacon Hill, it was difficult to follow a car. If one car got in between and decided to park, or let someone else in front of them, the quarry could easily get away. Yet, you'd get burned if you got too close.

I opted to let the Caddy go up a block and turn left before I raced the old van up to the corner and peeked around. This game of cat-and-mouse went on for three blocks, when the Caddy went through a yellow light. The light turned red before I got there. As the Caddy got a block up and began taking a right, I flashed my lights and crept through the intersection, cars honking, headlights flashing back at me, drivers shouting and showing me the finger. I yelled "Medical emergency!" stomped on the gas pedal, skidded around the next right, and there, ahead of me, was the Cadillac.

Up two more blocks, a left, and the Caddy pulled up to a corner space. The corner was diagonally across from Joe Panetta's apartment building. I wondered who the Fat Man might know in this neighborhood. I looked around for another restaurant.

The two thugs got out of the car and walked across the street and into Joe's apartment building. I was in a mild state of shock which was quickly turning into panic as Skinny and Ray-Bob looked out through the third floor hallway window, just a few feet from the Bean Counter's apartment door. Reno flashed the Caddy headlights. The scanner crackled as Reno put his phone to his face. I heard Reno's voice—it sounded like it came through a sewer pipe.

"Hello, Mr. Panetta?"

I felt the blood drain from my face.

"Jack Kelly sent me to pick up the ledger, the book he left with you. He's in a bit of a jam. He told me to tell you it was all right."

I couldn't believe the boldness of the plan. How did he know? Where had he gotten my accountant's phone number? I had told no one that Joe had the book. Maybe Ray-Bob had intercepted a message on my office answering machine.

I froze the scanner on that frequency. I hoped their simple plan was not going to work. I heard Reno talking.

"Yes, yes, well, no. He can't. I can't get him on the phone...I didn't want to tell you this, Mr. Panetta, but Jack's down at headquarters answering questions, and he thinks some book will save his ass. What? Those are two of my detectives knocking on your door, Mr. Panetta. You can check their identification, but unless you want to be booked for obstructing justice, you'll hand over that leather ledger! Now!"

I don't think the Bean Counter bought Reno's impression of what a detective should sound like. Even from a block back, I could hear Reno swearing as the line went dead. Reno flashed the headlights of the Cadillac into the descending darkness again. I knew this was meant to be a signal to Reno's goons to go ahead, break down the door if they have to, and take the book.

I felt the reassuring, heavyweight butt of my .45 as I stepped out of the van. This situation was getting out of control. I ran down the side of the street to where Reno sat in the car. I reached inside the open window and stuck the barrel of my gun just under his nose.

"Call it off Reno! If the accountant gets hurt, you'll pay the price! I promise you."

For a moment, he sat with his mouth open, in shock. Then he hit re-dial as fast as his chubby fingers could fly. I heard the busy signal and ran across the street, knowing Reno was too fat to follow or attack from the rear.

I didn't feel guilty about calling him Fat Boy anymore.

Just as I got to the front of the apartment building, I heard the sound of breaking glass coming from the rear. I was hoping I would see Joe Panetta flying down the back porch stairs as I headed to the alley around back.

As I looked up, I saw Joe flying down, but he wasn't using the stairs. He hit the cement sidewalk like a watermelon, with a sickening thud. One of those bastards had thrown my friend out of the third-floor window.

As I knelt down beside him he gasped, gurgled, spit up some blood, and thrust the book into my arms. I looked into his eyes as blood trickled from his nostrils and mouth. I shook my head.

"No, I don't care about that damn book anymore, Joe."

He shoved the book into my chest and looked at me hard. I knew what he would have said if his lungs and throat weren't filling with blood. He wanted to say "Goddamn it, Jack! Take this! I stood up for this. I took a stand! Don't let it be for nothing!"

The light in his eyes was fading, the last few moments of life were draining away.

The first shot cracked like slow motion thunder, the crack of floorboards crashing through, or a large tree breaking in half in a storm. The crack of a large caliber weapon discharging. Like the crack of a broken heart.

The bullet went deep into Joe's chest, hitting the bones of the rib cage and spine, causing his body to jerk. This poor, unfortunate human being I had dragged into this little war. This noble soldier for truth, justice, and the American Way.

I looked up from the sidewalk to the third-floor window, and saw Ray-Bob aiming a handgun at me. I clutched the book, and as I turned to run, I saw the Cadillac's headlights rapidly covering the distance between us. I jumped to the side and the black Cadillac screeched past, running over Joe with its front tires.

CHAPTER 28

The Mexican Standoff

Two more quick shots rang out.

The first struck the hood of the Caddy, releasing steam from the radiator. I didn't look back to see where the second hit, but I felt a small chunk of concrete hit the back of my leg. I ran left, then darted to the right. I ducked into the alley behind the Bean Counter's apartment building as the Fat Man jockeyed for a position to strike with the car. As I glanced back, I saw the front wheels of the Cadillac back over Joe's lifeless body for the second time.

I had run into a dead end alley, maybe two-hundred yards long, with brick walls on both sides. I knew it was a dead end, but I needed cover fast from the shooter on the third floor. But this was typical of me—a dead end alley.

There was no way out. This was not a dream I would wake up from. The headlights of the Caddy blinded me as Reno hit the high beams. The vehicle raced toward the alley entrance. Through the glare of the headlights, I could still see Reno behind the wheel, grinning, beads of sweat on his forehead, his dark eyes popping out with delight. My eyes darted left and right, up and down, looking for some avenue of escape.

As the speeding Cadillac entered the alley, I instinctively ran back about twenty yards. I turned and drew my gun up in line with the driver's head. It caused a rapid change in the expression in the rolls of fat that made up Reno's enormous face.

He turned the wheel to the right and the big car hit the wall, but it kept on coming, its fenders and side panels screeching, windows popping, and sparks flying. The Cadillac, grinding up against the alley wall, began slowing. I jumped straight up as the car slid in underneath me. I landed on the hood with my weapon still trained on

Mr. Big's fat head as the Caddy screeched, crunched, and ground to a stop.

The moment seemed suspended in time. Reno and I looked at each other. The radiator hissed, shooting steam straight up into the air. The smell of burnt rubber, and smoke from the right front tire, drifted upward. Glass from the windows still rained down, landing on the roof, hood, and ground. A rolling hubcap clattered on down the alleyway, finally circling a few times, and clanging to rest. Then there was silence. I was still focused on the piece of garbage at the end of my gun sights.

I was thinking about my chances of being acquitted in a self-defense shooting when Ray-Bob and Skinny came around the corner, their guns drawn.

"Tell them to back off now, Fatman, or they'll be looking for a refrigerator box to bury you in!"

"Get back! Get back!" Reno hollered.

"Get out of the car!" I shouted back at him. I was large and in charge, standing on the hood of the Cadillac, his precious book in my left hand and a .45 in my right. And I didn't care anymore.

The Big Man was struggling to get out of the car. He was really getting on my nerves. He was inching his butt across the seat towards the driver's door. He was grunting, groaning, and attempting to pull himself up using the car door. I gave him some more incentive.

"Move it, Fats or I'll kill you right now! You didn't have to hurt the Bean Counter! And you've been trying to hurt me. Move it! Go ahead! Just try something. You want to, don't you? Go ahead! Let's settle this right now!"

By now Reno was moving quickly for a big fellow. His eyes were wide open, his mouth gasping for air. He got to his feet and put his hands in the air as he began his little birdlike walk out of the alley. Ray-Bob and Skinny looked on in shock, standing in the intersection as Reno and I walked toward them. From behind I whispered into Reno's ear as we walked.

"Tell them to put the guns away, or I'll put one in the back of your fat head. And put your hands down!"

"Put the guns away! Right now! Put them away!" Reno groaned and garbled, his voice strained and shaking.

I had Reno at the business end of a gun, and I liked it. I needed some questions answered—like what the hell was this all about? Why had Bella and Reno's sideshow come to my office? Had Reno sent me the package? How did it tie in with the serial killer? It was time I dealt directly with the source of my pain—Reno.

The sound of sirens in the distance, coming from several directions, brought me back to reality. As we stood in the intersection on Beacon Hill, I could almost hear the whir of minds spinning. Obviously, Reno and friends didn't want to be there when the cops arrived. I was thinking that I didn't either. I had a gun on these three, and the approaching officers could construe it as a life-threatening situation. They were probably responding to a report of gunshots, and I was holding a gun. They could commit an act of justifiable homicide by firing on me.

Other thoughts began to race through my mind. What if these three "witnesses" told a story that made me out to be an out of control gunman? That wouldn't be a hard picture to paint. By the time formal statements were made, I was sure they'd try to pin the Bean Counter's murder on me.

Reno stared back at me with a grotesque grin as the sirens grew louder and my resolve grew weaker.

"Reno!" I used my command voice. "Come over here with me. We've got to talk."

I had made up my mind. I had to leave the area. With the odds stacked against me, I couldn't afford to have Reno, his witnesses, and his friends "upstairs" put a negative spin on the evening's events. I didn't want to get arrested at the murder scene. I imagined being molded into the perpetrator, even being charged with robbing Fat Boy of the book. I could imagine some rookie handing it to him as they took me away in handcuffs.

As I walked Reno around the corner at gunpoint, I heard the scurrying steps of Ray-Bob and Skinny fleeing in the opposite direction. My plan was working.

"Reno, we've got unfinished business. I haven't figured out what this is all about yet, but you're dirty. You stink bad, Reno. And you're going to go down. Turn around and walk out into that street. Go ahead and walk towards the accountant. Move! Look at him as you walk over to him. And don't stop until I tell you!"

I'm a sensitive guy, but I don't feel too badly about calling him Fats, Butterballs, or Mr. Big Chunk anymore.

The sirens were getting louder as I backed up and Reno waddled slowly towards Joe's body lying in the street. I slipped into the van and backed out and up the street into the dark with my lights off, just as the first cruiser arrived.

CHAPTER 29

The Right Thing To Do

My mind was racing as I drove across and down the side of Beacon Hill. My hands were still shaking. I wasn't sure. Was I fleeing a murder scene? Was I really a suspect in several of the serial killings?

For the moment I was alone, safe, and mobile. I had avoided being shot or run over, and I wasn't in police custody. Wasn't my first obligation to secure my own safety? Even at the Police Academy, we were taught that the first priority was officer safety. That included getting to a safe area and then dealing with the problem.

I wondered what Reno would say after being caught at the scene of a murder. It was his big ass in the ringer now—a dead man—a body damaged beyond repair, a report of gunshots, a Cadillac probably registered to Reno crunched up in the alley.

But a friend of mine was dead because I'd involved him. I just couldn't go on with business as usual. I couldn't let The Fat Man tell the story. At first, I thought by leaving him at the scene, I was leaving him holding the bag. But the more I thought about it, I may have made him and his boys the sole witnesses to the events transpiring, including the flight of the Bean Counter. If the Chunky One tells a story that features this red haired, blue eyed, private investigator, I could be up for another murder.

The Trash Man was supposed to have "connections at the top," and he might convince the initial officer and subsequent investigators of my involvement. It wouldn't be the first time law enforcement jumped to a conclusion around here. The Boston Strangler, that other noted local serial killer, who killed 13 women between 1962 and 1964, was said to be Albert DeSalvo, a Malden factory worker. But there are many in law enforcement that say it wasn't him. He was not only never convicted but not even charged with the string of strangulations perpetrated in the Boston area. He was convicted of sexual assaults and armed robbery and sentenced to life in prison, where he was stabbed to death in 1973.

I had to go back. Or turn myself in. Or at least call Bill Rogers at homicide, or Detective Houston of the State Police.

I was sure with all the gunshots, bodies crashing out windows, and a Cadillac hitting a wall, witnesses from the usually quiet Beacon Hill neighborhood would be emerging to tell police of a madman with dark red hair kneeling by a body in the street, or standing on the hood of a Cadillac pointing a gun at Thaddeus Reno and screaming, "I'll kill you right now!"

I had to go back. I turned the old blue van around and headed back up Beacon Hill the way I had just come. I hoped some cop wouldn't see me and try to make a daring capture by putting a couple of rounds into my head.

I headed back. I felt good about it, too. I knew I was doing the right thing. As I rounded the corner and drove down the block to the crime scene, I knew returning with the book was the right thing to do. I was an innocent man, a detective, caught up in a web of intrigue.

I parked the van in the same spot I had parked before and walked towards the lights of the intersection. Maybe I was feeding the faith and starving the doubt, but I felt good about doing the right thing, bringing everything out into the light.

As I walked into the lights of the intersection: streetlights, headlights, and arc lights set up for the crime scene photographers, I saw Joe lying on the ground.

I looked toward a small group of young policeman, standing in a circle. In the center of the group I saw a pretty, blonde-haired, EMT working on Reno as he sat on a stretcher. He was the center of attention, the star of the show. As I neared, I heard his guttural voice, like the sound of a garbage disposal through a sewer pipe.

"The gun looked soooo big, like a cannon. And the deranged look in his eyes. Then he took my car and ran over that poor man. And then he threatened to kill me!"

Reno and I made eye contact. I smiled and held up the book. His expression changed rapidly from a look of bemused delight to an expression of horror. I was doing the right thing.

"There's the maniac with the gun!" Reno screamed.

As the circle parted and all eyes were on me, Reno reached down, and pulled out the officer's gun who was standing next to him, and shot me, once in the chest.

No, this was not the right thing to do.

CHAPTER 30

Dead Bodies

The first dead body I remember seeing, I was six years old. Me and my friend Pendy went to the movie theater down on the avenue. We had seen "I Was A Teenage Werewolf" starring Michael Landon. We were leaving the theater, and we saw a group of people forming a circle across the street on the corner. We were walking in that direction, and we slowly crossed the street. Being little kids at that time, we crawled right under the crowd, to get a look at what everyone was looking at.

On the sidewalk lay a man with gray hair and skin to match. One look, and we knew he was dead. He wasn't moving. He wasn't breathing. He was pale and sickly. His eyes were open, but the inner light had been extinguished. He was dead. We watched him being put into the ambulance and being taken away.

I hadn't given much thought to death. All I knew was what I had seen in the movies—like when a cowboy gets shot off his horse or dies in a gunfight. Maybe a spaceship gets blown up, a spaceman gets vaporized by a ray gun, or an army guy falls on a grenade to save his friend. Maybe death was the ultimate justice, the final reward, when a gangster gets machine gunned, or a monster throws a scientist off a cliff.

They say your life passes before your eyes when you die. Your life's like a movie. Then the end. Game over.

We cringe from death. We shrink from death. We don't want to discuss it. We don't want to think about the inevitable death of our loved ones. And the inevitable death of ourselves.

As a cop I'd seen all kinds of death—sudden deaths, car accidents, gunshot wounds, overdoses, murder victims. Old folks, five days stale, dead infants, their life over before it starts. Shotgun suicides with pieces of brain and skull imbedded in the ceiling, blood still oozing from the face. Sometimes the bodies looked like they were made out of wax. Or like a mannequin.

The cop sees it all. He or she may handle the situation very business-like, but they see what has happened. They may be writing reports and asking questions but don't think it doesn't effect them.

I heard about a cop who would go to the scene of a death, especially unattended deaths, would bring a Polaroid camera and take a shot with the stiff. He would pose with it. He would prop up the body, put some sunglasses on it's face, a cigarette in it's mouth, maybe a hat on it's head, and hold up the dead guy's arm like he was waving. And take a picture of himself with his arm around the stiff. That's just this one deranged guy. I've heard he has a wall full of these pictures.

A cop would never do that on a homicide or other case when evidence shouldn't be disturbed. But when a death has been ruled simply as unattended or death by natural causes and the cop has to stay with the body until someone from the funeral parlor arrives and takes the body away, it can be hours, depending on the time of day or night. It's a bizarre situation, standing around with a corpse lying on the floor or on the bed.

And the funeral parlors—God knows what they do to them. The morticians make a neck incision and another inside the thigh, then pump in fluids that de-coagulates blood. They pump out and drain the blood and other fluids and replace them with formaldehyde and alcohol solutions. Maybe some Perma-Glo embalming fluid for that just dead look. They take a bunch of things out—internal organs, intestines—then pack a bunch of stuff back in, newspapers and hay they used to use, filling the body cavities, and stitch up any gaping holes or incisions. Some funeral parlors bring in a hairdresser. Maybe a haircut or a shave. Glue the eyes shut. Maybe they'll put a few cotton balls in their cheeks. A little perfume. Then put makeup on their face, dress them up in their Sunday best, and lay them out. Quite ghoulish.

Why do we do the things we do?

The thought of death has a strong effect. It is powerful. Life altering. It has deep psychological meaning.

Now it had a deep personal reality for me.

CHAPTER 31

The Last Nightmare

It started the same way it always did. The clouds began to roll backwards, slowly imploding and exploding. The light seemed uncertain and grew dimmer. My timing was just a little off. My feet weren't sure under me. The air seemed dense, a little thicker, harder to suck in, and even harder to hear through. I wasn't sure where I was.

My legs seemed to get heavier and my feet sank as I walked on. Even my thoughts seemed to grow muddy, thick, and slow. Like in quicksand, the harder I tried to move, the more bogged down I became.

I soon became aware of something I already knew. Something was stalking me. Some thing was tracking me. Moving closer, closing the distance between us. It could see me, sense me, and it kept on coming, following a trail in the dark towards me.

It was relentless, single minded, and focused. Closing the distance. It was merciless. It enjoyed hunting me, as if it were some kind of pay back. Mankind getting some pay back for all the animals that have been stalked, hunted, and killed.

I knew I was in a rut with this dream. It had been a recurring nightmare with me for about three years. I knew it was about control—or the lack of it, in my case. I knew I panicked when I couldn't have absolute control over everything around me. I knew this dream was an illustration, an attempt to teach me to surrender to fate, or at least turn to face the light at the end of the tunnel even if it was an onrushing train.

I strained to pick up each leg and move forward, even as I sensed it coming up behind me. I could hear the thick underbrush crunching under its weight. The air began to fill with the stench of it, like something dead, rotting in a sewer by the roadside. I could hear its breath hiss and its throat growl through it's salivating drool. I knew it was grinning and snickering. It was coming up behind me.

In the past when I had the dream I'd always run and run, and tried to get away. And I always struggled and fought as hard as I could. I wouldn't look at it. I never surrendered.

But now I was beyond the fear of fate dealing me a bad hand. It seemed simple now. Bad hand? That was a laugh. Fate had been dragging me over hot coals. When I woke up the nightmare began! Suspected murderer. I had spent my life solving crime and helping to bring the bad to justice. I had never crossed the line. That had to be good for something.

Maybe I'd just cash in my chips. I wasn't afraid of fate anymore. Maybe I'd take a stand. I was clean, lean and mean, like a boxer who had trained hard. Trained through adversity. Tempered by contact. Weathered by the storm. I could suck it up and last into the late rounds. And maybe I'd still be standing.

I felt the hot breath on the back of my neck, its stench filled the air around me. It had never been this close before. As it raised its head and roared, I knew I wasn't going to outrun it, and I didn't want to. I stopped in my tracks then slowly turned around and looked straight into the face of my fears. My legs were quivering. My whole body shook. My eyes felt as if they would pop out from fear. As I turned, I saw its amorphous shape, changing before me, rearing its head, rising to attack.

I reached back under my left arm with my right hand and felt the butt of my .45 caliber Colt Combat Commander. I couldn't believe it was there. I pulled the gun out and leveled it, center mass. The expression on its face changed dramatically, just as the Fat Man's face had changed earlier when I'd pointed the gun barrel at his head. I pumped two rounds into the center of its mass, and it began to howl in excruciating pain. Another shot to the face. There was smoke and muzzle flash as each rapid fire and devastating boom cracked. Then I began emptying the clip into it.

The air was filled with gun smoke and gut wrenching wails and moans as steaming gasses were released from its hideous form. Shot after shot. It was agonizing. Ten shots. It was hurt. I dropped one clip out and shoved in another. Faster and faster, the automatic punched out the bullets. Fifteen. Thirty shots. Fifty. One hundred.

It was dying. The automatic just kept firing and firing.

CHAPTER 32

Off At Code H

The bright hospital lights blinded me as I struggled on the hospital bed, struggled to wake to the nightmare of reality. Was it over? Was I dead yet?

Two nurses and a policeman held my arms and legs. The voices began to filter in.

"Please, don't move. You're going to hurt yourself."

"It's all right, it's all right." I heard the soothing female voices say.

My eyes began to focus. I began to realize I was off at Code H. When I worked patrol and I was going to stop off at the hospital, protocol dictated I say, "I'll be off at Code H" over the radio. We were off at Code H a lot—accident victims, domestic abuse victims, injured prisoners, overdoses.

I was in a bright hospital room with the two nurses and a uniformed police officer. It was dark outside the windows. I was hot and sweating. I couldn't remember why I was there, at first. The older nurse said, "People often have seizures when there is an entrance and an exit wound."

I tried to say something, but I just grunted. My mouth was dry and felt like it was filled with paste or cotton. Slowly, the recollection that I had been shot in the chest came back. At first I didn't recall how. Then I remembered Reno pointing the gun at me as the crowd of police officers parted. I remembered the crack of thunder as the cannon shot. I remember getting knocked down by a hit in the chest from an invisible sledgehammer.

I took a deep breath and felt the pain on the left side of my chest shoot all the way through to the left side of my back. "What?" I managed to stammer.

"Well…" the young nurse began. Then she looked at the big, gray-haired beat officer now standing by the door. He shook his head. I wondered if he was there to keep people out or to keep me in.

The older nurse spoke up. "Jack, you were shot last night, and brought here to Mass General by ambulance. It was touch and go for awhile—your blood pressure went up and down. They thought they had lost you. The doctors operated on you yesterday. You've been out all day. As I understand it, the bullet went right through you, but there was a lot of repair work to do. The doctor will tell you the details. Now I'm going to take your blood pressure and temperature and give you a shot so you can get some rest."

I lay still as they went about their routine. I was coming around slowly. Bits and pieces began cascading into my bleary consciousness. Then the young nurse administered a syringe into a port in one of the intravenous lines that ran into a tube stuck in the top of my hand. I stared into her beautiful hazel eyes. I began to drift, and my eyes closed.

This time I began drifting towards the warmth and security of Johnny's place, the nightclub of my dreams. The familiar surroundings, a tiny world of its own, a dreamy microcosm of urban nightlife, here on planet earth. The place where my friends were hanging out, listening to jazz and blues.

There were things I needed to know, but at that moment I needed to drift, to relax, to let go...and float downstream.

CHAPTER 33

The Light

The sunlight flooded my hospital room as I awoke to the sounds of a nurse shuffling around. It was a bright morning, a new day, and a fresh chance to put everything into perspective and be done with it. That's pretty optimistic for a guy with a couple of holes in him. I had other events to attend to in my life.

The older nurse put two more pillows under my head. She was quite good-looking, even though there was a space you could park a small car in between her top front teeth. She gave me some juice to sip through a straw, and I was glad to have it. She came to my bedside with another syringe but I declined, mumbling something about needing a clear head. I did take the five or six pills the doctor had ordered for me.

"What do you know about me? Why is there a policeman outside the door?" I asked.

She didn't indicate a thing. Even her facial expressions told me nothing. I asked her if there was a newspaper around. No response. I asked if she could turn on the television that was blankly staring down at me suspended from the ceiling. She scowled. I asked if there was a telephone in the room. No response. As she finished her assigned tasks and headed for the door, I spoke up a little more forcefully.

"So, just let me ask you one more thing!"

She stopped and looked at me like a third grade math teacher about to deal with an unruly child.

I spoke coyly, blinking my eyes frequently. "Do you think a girl should put out on the first date, or should she wait until the second?"

A thin crack of a smile broke her stoic face. She broke out into a full, gapped-toothed smile and walked out the door saying, "Why don't you ask your fiancée`? She's been waiting in the visitors' lounge for two days."

I would have jumped right out of bed if I could have. Of course my girlfriend was there. She was waiting nearby. There were people who cared about me.

We had met many years before on one of my first cases. She was being stalked, and hired me to investigate. This stalker fit the profile very well. He was in his middle thirty's, he was intelligent, but had a psychiatric history and was a substance abuser. He had mood disorders, some criminal history, and most importantly, a string of failed relationships, sexual and otherwise. Failure was the lot, for this obsessed follower.

The crime of stalking is very much on the rise. Most stalkers are male. Some stalkers eventually kill the object of their attention. This one almost killed my client. She later became my lover and girlfriend. But, that's another story.

After spending one minute with her, I wanted to stalk her, too. Those big, big, green eyes, and long straight auburn hair. She was the wholesome, girl-next-door type, but with a body that didn't quit. And she had class. You could see it in the way she carried herself. She's from a poor but honest family of Irish-Italian descent. Maybe she's a little naive, more trusting than I, but who isn't? In her eyes, I'm her Blue Knight.

The same stoic nurse, who was now smiling, came back through the door, and told me, "The doctor says you can see your fiancée` for a few minutes."

I was wondering when she began to refer to herself as my fiancée`? As the nurse ducked back out, the ghost of Bella Pavoni walked in.

My thoughts raced as I leaned back farther into my hospital bed in horror. I felt helpless as she walked toward me. I must be dreaming again, but it felt real. As my eyes nearly popped out of my head, the ghost spoke.

"I 'm Maria Pavoni, Bella's sister. I'm sorry, but they told me the only persons who could visit you had to be relatives. There was a pretty girl with long dark hair waiting for you all day, but she left before you woke up. I told them I was your fiancée. I hope you'll forgive me. I'm so sorry, Jack! Your getting shot had something to do with Bella, didn't it?"

I was slowly coming out of shock. She looked strikingly like Bella—the long legs, thin waist, large chest, full red lips, the dazzling blue eyes, and the short, jet-black hair.

"Are you twins?"

"No, just sisters. Bella is...was...fourteen months older than me."

"How did you know I was here?" I asked as I regained what little composure I had left.

"It's on television and in the papers. That Gordon Little, the reporter for WBZ, was interviewing a policeman, there on Beacon Hill. The video shows you walking in, the cops and other people stepping back, then Reno pulling out the cop's gun and shooting you. You fell straight back to the ground."

"That would explain the pain and the large bump on the back of my head."

"Jack, does this have something to do with Bella?"

"Yeah. I got tied into this when Bella came to my office that night. She never even told me what she wanted from me. She said she needed help. She didn't even have time to tell me the problem before the traveling sideshow of the Two-Ton Man and his midget showed up. Guns were pulled, and I got pistol-whipped. The next morning I was looking at the woman who had looked to me for help, dead in a rail car, her neck snapped, her eyes staring back at me, as if to say, `Where the hell were you when I needed you?'"

Maria began to cry softly.

"I'm sorry, Maria. I should've been more tactful."

"It's all right, Jack. I want to know," Maria said.

She walked over to the window, looked out across Storrow Drive eight floors below. The full moon reflected off of the Charles River.

"Does this have something to do with a leather-bound book?"

"What do you know about it?" I demanded, wondering for the first time where the book was now. Even though I wasn't sure what the book was, I knew if Reno had it back, he could cut his losses and run.

"Bella and Reno used to go to this nightclub near South Station all the time. The Channel. Reno would sit at a table in the back and do all kinds of business deals. He would meet people, talk on his phone, and eat constantly. Food was brought in from all over the city. He would send guys out to pick up fruit from the Haymarket, pasta from the North End, Chinese food, seafood from the best restaurants, big trays of sushi from The Genji on Newbury Street. He was nuts with the food. It was like a party, only he'd be doing business all the time. He would put over all kinds of business deals by wining and dining his associates. Bella talked about it all the time. She was quite impressed with him at first."

I watched Maria closely and said nothing.

"I went there with Bella a few times," she continued. "See, Reno had her thinking she was going to be a big-time famous singer. He was going to make it happen. He set up some time in a recording studio downtown to make a demo tape with a big-time producer. He bought her a back-up band. This weird transvestite guy, Digby Riggs, the one who plays at the nightclub, ran the band for Reno. They rehearsed there during the day. Even though the band was supposed to be Bella's, Reno paid all the bills."

"They rehearsed at The Channel?" I asked.

"That's the place."

"What do you know about the book? The leather-covered ledger?"

"Well, Bella told me everything was going along really good. Reno was getting richer and richer. He was becoming a real wheeler-dealer who always had a phone stuck to his ear. He was getting in, I mean, with the big politicians, you know? The Lieutenant Governor was meeting with him, and they were making some kind of big business deals. Reno's business was getting tax breaks and subsidies. They even met at The Channel on a night when Bella brought me along, almost two months ago.

"It was that night Reno got really upset, and knocked over the table with all his food on it. He was raging. It was something about a set of leather bound business books. Bella told me a trusted accountant with Reno's garbage business had made a list of all Reno's major accounts and what they were supposed to be paying. Then he listed what they actually paid, a sum much higher over a period of time. This accountant was a childhood friend of Reno's. Thaddeus turned all red and the veins in his neck and face bulged out, you know? The accountant was asking for a lot of money for the book so he could retire to a sailboat in Aruba or somewhere. Reno was furious. Bella said the accountant was going to turn the book over to a special investigator for the state, you know, if he didn't get paid off right away. Reno said he'd never pay."

I was wondering how this beautiful girl had come into my life from out of nowhere, and how she knew more than me about what the hell was going on.

"Jack, you look tired," Maria said.

"Don't stop, Maria, please go on."

"Well, I don't really know anything, but that was one of the nights the Lieutenant Governor came to The Channel. He met Reno at his table in the back lounge. He ate some, drank a little, and talked a lot with Reno. Bella said that if the book went to a state investigator, Lieutenant Governor King would try to get it back before copies were made. Reno told him he had to get it back or King was going to go down with him. I guess once you were in bed with Reno, well, he didn't like anybody leaving, you know? Not even an important man like the Lieutenant Governor. Reno treated Bella like she was a possession. God, I hope she never slept with that walrus." Maria made a face, and her body shook as if she had swallowed some vinegar. I liked her.

A different nurse, an Asian lady who reminded me of a little oriental doll, and an orderly with some food had come into the room. The nurse was going through her routine of putting the food within arm's reach of me and straightening up the room for a minute before she approached me with the cup of assorted pills. I dutifully swallowed the half dozen in one gulp, and washed them down with orange juice.

"You're a good boy then, aren't you?" the nurse chirped in a slightly British accent as she watched appreciatively.

"How do I know you're a nurse here? You could be an assassin."

"Well, you've already taken the pills, now haven't you? If you die, then you'll know I wasn't your nurse."

"Everybody's a comedian."

"Only a few more minutes, please, miss." The oriental doll left, taking the orderly with her.

"Maria, what are the TV and papers saying? Am I under arrest, in protective custody, or what?"

"I don't know exactly. There is a policeman outside your door. The newspaper said police were waiting to question you. They didn't say you had been arrested. I don't think you're going anyplace soon. The story I read was headlined something like 'BEACON HILL MURDER AND SHOOTING PROBED.'"

"Yeah, I guess I'm not going anywhere. The DA likes to get all his ducks in a row before he lines up his shotgun."

"Jack, you haven't done anything...have you?"

"Well, no. Except that I haven't exactly come forward, even though I might've known they were looking for me. They could hang something on me. I get the feeling they'll try to." I wasn't usually so pessimistic, but the streak of bad luck that had brought me to that point was probably not over.

"But I do know Reno has been put under arrest."

"What?" I croaked with amazement. Then my brain engaged. "Oh, of course! For shooting poor me!"

I hadn't even thought of that. The shock was wearing off. The pieces were finally coming together, the picture coming into focus. I tried to get up but a dull pain shot through my chest. I laid back down. The drugs were beginning to take effect.

"Take it easy, Jack," Maria said sympathetically. She put her hand on my shoulder and slowly and gently rubbed. I was staring up into her cobalt blue eyes, beginning to drift. I was thinking that this could be the end of the worst time of my life...and the beginning of a beautiful friendship.

I was unwinding so fast I didn't even see the three men in suits enter my room. Maria saw them first, and realized her time was up. The detectives wanted to speak to me alone. She said she would come back in the morning. I thanked her and asked her to bring a newspaper.

Detective Sergeant Jeff Houston of the State Police, Sergeant Bill Rogers from Boston Homicide, and my friend Sergeant Jim Watson, stood over me, looking, without speaking for what seemed like a long time.

"Jack, you don't have to say anything now," Houston said. The detective sergeant was clean- with a small black mole under his right eye and wore his straight brown hair on the longish side for a cop. He was six -foot four and about two hundred and thirty pounds. His voice sounded like thunder in the distance as he towered over me.

"I'm not even going to read you Miranda until tomorrow morning. At that time, I'm going to want to ask you some questions, and you can make a statement at that time. How are you feeling?"

"Ups and downs, sir." If he was advising me to not say anything about the murder of the accountant, then I was taking his advice.

"Jack, you'll be glad to know we have Reno," Rogers said. "He's being charged with the aggravated assault on you. Maybe even attempted murder. He'll need to have a really expensive lawyer to get him off on this. One of those dirtbag lawyers that can get a rape charge reduced to tailgating. Even if he says he was afraid for his life, or whatever. And we're trying to verify his story about you pushing Panetta out the window."

"What?" I screamed. I tried to get up, but Jim Watson stepped up and held my shoulders.

"Don't hurt yourself, Jack," Jim said as he looked back at Sergeant Houston. "Not all of us believe the garbage Reno is selling. Not everybody is falling in line with the pressure from upstairs, or downtown."

"Watch it, Jim," Houston piped in.

"A couple of the guys are working your angle, Jack," Jim tried to reassure me.

The Trash Man was setting me up for Joe's death. If he had killed me, he would've stuck the whole mess on me.

"Where's the book?" I asked the general population of my hospital room.

The puzzled expression on the faces of the three detectives sent a shock wave through my aching body.

"The ledger I was carrying when Reno shot me? In front of a dozen policemen!" My voice was getting louder. The uniformed cop outside my door poked his head in. Houston waved him back out.

Bill Rogers said, "The clothes you were wearing, your gun, and I believe the large book you were carrying, have all been entered into evidence. The lab guys are going over your clothes and gun."

"Don't lose that ledger. And don't let Reno get his hands on it, Sarge. It's the key to this and possibly other murders."

I could see my words had the proper effect on the detectives. Maybe they wouldn't turn the book over to Reno even if he claimed it as his property.

"Jack, let's not say any more at this time. Tomorrow we'll start from the beginning, with the Assistant District Attorney, and get it all down. I can see we've got a long way to start straightening things out here," Houston said.

I wondered if he was looking to nail me.

I was yawning and I felt like my eyes were crossing. The nurse had evidently given me something in one of the pills I'd taken. I told the detectives I wasn't going anywhere, and I wanted to clear this whole matter as soon as possible. Jim Watson squeezed my hand and told me he was glad I was alive. I thought I saw the makings of a tear in the old detective's eye.

"You get some rest, Jack," he said.

"Yeah, if I get tired of doing nothing, I'll stop and rest," I said as they walked toward the door.

As the veiled curtain of sleep began overtaking me, I saw the detectives slip out of the room. The muffled voices and footsteps in the hall grew faint. I began to drift.

231

CHAPTER 34

Dead Serious

They transported him to jail handcuffed in the back of a police wagon, I was told. He couldn't fit in the back of a cruiser. They didn't have a place for a man of Reno's extreme size at the old and cramped Charles Street Jail, so the cops took him to the big holding tank at the D Street Police Station in Southie. It was an old brick precinct headquarters and had a big holding cell, a drunk tank, just off the lobby.

Reno had apparently complained of his discomfort, proclaimed his innocence, and demanded his lawyer be brought to him immediately upon his arrival. Of course, he threatened to sue everybody. After he was photographed and fingerprinted, he was allowed to make a call to his lawyer to start the ball rolling towards his release.

But the bail on somebody who shoots a cop, or in my case an ex-cop, was always very high. Even considering Reno's wealth, it was going to take some time to put that kind of package together.

Reno spent his time complaining, whining, moaning and groaning, and from what I heard he didn't sleep at all that first night. Probably because he had none of his creature comforts—no access to large quantities of gourmet food, no telephone to order up the many delicacies that he required, no communication with his goon squad, I mean, business associates, no customized bathroom to accommodate a man of his size, and no specially made bed to allow a six-hundred and fifty-plus pound man room to toss and turn.

He did eat every scrap of food they gave him, though, and had apparently attempted bribery to get more. He needed to feed his various habits. He wasn't adjusting well. I guess that's when he got the idea.

The Huge One clutched his chest and fell down on the floor. The way I heard it, Reno worked himself into quite a state, rolling around, gasping for air, like he was having the big one. While an officer, Jennings, balked at performing CPR on the behemoth, the desk sergeant called for a rescue unit, telling them to bring some extra manpower for a man close to seven feet tall and weighing nearly seven-hundred pounds.

CHAPTER 35

The Tube

I slowly became aware there were people scuffling around in the room. Bright lights were being turned on. As I struggled to peer out from my still drooping eyelids, I could see the young nurse from yesterday setting up a stainless steel table by my bed with fresh bandages, towels, tape, and some reddish antiseptic-type fluids in three squeeze bottles.

A clean cut, baby-faced young man who looked about nineteen years old and wearing green hospital scrubs approached me. He told me he was a doctor and was going to clean and dress my wound after the nurse took my vitals. This was not the way I preferred to wake up.

"What time is it? It's not even light out yet." I said.

"Ten past five," said the Teen Doc.

The doctor—he said his name was Tad or Todd—took the old bloodied dressing off my chest. I don't have much hair on my chest, but when he pulled the adhesive tape off, even in quick movements, I felt the sting. This was good, I thought. I didn't even wince or cry out loud once. And then I looked down and saw the tube sticking out of my chest. There was a huge bruise on my chest around the end of the tube. I then realized why I had an uncomfortable spot on the left side of my back.

"Does that tube go all the way through me and out my back?" I asked, like a kid watching his science teacher performing an experiment.

"Yes. All the way through. I'll anesthetize you with some local shots of lidocaine, and we'll take out that stent, that tube, in a few minutes, while we clean out the wound channel."

The nurse took my vital signs, lowered the bed to flat, and proceeded to clean some dried blood around both ends of the tube while the doctor put his rubber gloves on. He stuck some needles into

236

the area around the tube. Then the kid doctor began squirting the reddish-colored liquid into the end of the tube. The liquid soon began to squirt out the other end, out of my back, onto towels and a flat tray the nurse had put down on the bed under my back. It was a bit uncomfortable, feeling the cool liquid running through my chest and out my back, but there was a certain feeling of progress.

The doctor asked the nurse for some assistance. He then proceeded to slowly, in short, smooth motions, begin pulling the tube out through my chest, while the nurse squirted fluids in and onto the tube. Even though I was anesthetized, I could feel the end of the tube slowly coming through my body. The liquids were cold and running inside the wound channel.

"I would've asked you to warm those fluids, Doc," I managed to say while holding my chest as still as I could. I would have asked him to knock me out, too.

He was all business. I felt the end of the tube inching its way from my back through my body and slowly exit out my chest. Then he pushed, squeezed, and molded on the area of my wounds as if he thought I was made out of clay, squeezing out as much fluid as possible. I groaned and grew a little lightheaded. While they were cleaning up the mess they had made, the doctor told me the facts about my condition.

"Well, if you've made it this far, I don't think you're going to die. The bullet narrowly missed any major organs, bones, lung, and main arteries. There may not be any permanent damage. We'll have to see about that. Right now, the nurse will remove the IV, we'll sew those openings up, and send you off to x-ray. Hopefully we won't have to go back in."

I might not die, there may be no permanent damage, and they may not have to go back in. Well, that sounded reassuring.

After they sewed me up and I went through x-ray, an orderly rolled me back into my room. I was quite exhausted, and more than a bit sore. The old, stoic nurse came in with some toast, tea, and fruit juice. She offered me a choice of a syringe of morphine or some pills of a similar nature. I opted for the syringe. She seemed to enjoy the process of rolling me over and administering the syringe into my exposed rear end, and I thought I would take the opportunity to tease her a bit.

"Now that you've seen my bare ass, you'll have to marry me," I said.

She scowled. It was working.

"I've seen a lot of buttocks in my twenty-four years as a nurse, sir," she replied.

"But none as fine as mine, nurse. Come on, admit it. You're excited. It's the perfect pear shape, isn't it?"

She cracked a half smile, exposing the space between her teeth, blushed like a schoolgirl, slapped me on the ass, and headed for the door. As she was leaving, she turned, scowled, and said "Save it for one of your "fiancée's."

I took a few deep breaths and began to feel the morphine warming my body from head to toe. Outside my window, the sunlight was beginning to hit the sides of the buildings on this clear Boston morning.

Just then, my girlfriend stuck her head around the corner of the door. When she came into my hospital room, she lit it up like a Christmas tree. I was so glad to see her. She looked great. Her long brown hair falling over a brown pinstripe suit with a slit skirt. She had the sweetest smile, and her green eyes twinkled.

Her radiant smile soon turned to tears as she laid her head down on my chest and gave me a gentle but firm squeeze. I would have been deeply touched, had the pain not once again shot through my upper body.

"Oh, Jack!" she quietly sobbed. "Don't ever let this happen again! I can't take this again. I've missed you so much."

I planted some soft kisses on the back of her neck. I was getting a little choked up, too. My eyes began to tear up from the emotion I was experiencing and the pain I was feeling from her weight on my chest as she squeezed me. I was a sensitive guy.

"I didn't mean to hurt you, Bug Eyes. The bad man did this to me, Honey. The big, round, globular, overstuffed, mammoth, swollen, immense, colossal, huge, enormously…fat…"

By now she was looking at me and smiling.

"The bad man, Honey."

CHAPTER 36

Back From The Dead

After I slept for several hours, I woke to see my girlfriend still sitting on the edge of the bed, holding my hand.

She didn't know much about the case. The news covered the basics. The Bean Counter was murdered. I had been shot. Reno had been arrested.

I'll give a statement to the investigators later today. Then I hoped they would fill in some of the holes. And not arrest me.

She helped me eat a little of the hospital food. She had to spoon feed me. I could hardly even talk from the pain of the chest wound. We spent the next two hours together just holding hands. She talked about the normal, average, quiet things. I drifted off occasionally. Morphine was a nice place to visit, but I wouldn't want to live there.

I felt a small triumph when I was able to walk, slowly, to the bathroom. On my return I was greeted by the young doctor who seemed impressed by my journey. The doctor told me he had informed the three police detectives I could not make a statement until much later in the day, if at all. He told me I must have "complete rest" for the day. The young doctor very politely asked my girlfriend to leave, telling her she could stop back after 8 p.m. and she would be able to see me then.

"Angel, would you call my brother and ask him to be present when the good detectives return to question me? I'll see you soon, love."

She kissed me and they both left. And not a moment too soon. I was exhausted. Getting shot took a lot out of you. Rest sounded like a good plan to me. I knew I could drift right off to sleep. I was as safe and snug as a bug in a rug. I had doctors and nurses just a button call away. I had a cop right outside my door. Safe and sound. I couldn't be safer.

CHAPTER 37

The Snapper

I later found out that while I was feeling safe and secure in the private room section of the hospital on the eighth floor, the ambulance carrying The Fat Man arrived silently at the Mass General Emergency Room doors. No sirens are allowed near the hospital. A Boston Police car pulled up and parked in the No Parking zone. Four brawny officers got out and walked to the rear of the ambulance. Along with the two ambulance attendants, the six men carried the enormously heavy weight of Thaddeus Reno into the Emergency Room.

Big, fat Thaddeus Reno should have been taken to Boston City Hospital, where all the city's inmates went, but Reno was thought to have heart trouble. Inmates with heart problems went to Mass General, where the facilities and specialists for a cardiac case reside.

It was early evening, and Reno was sitting up in his bed in the ER, watching television and finishing off his second tray of hospital food. The doctors hadn't found anything wrong with Reno—nothing other than his normally overtaxed heart. The staff had prescribed something to calm his excited heart, but Reno had been covertly spitting the pills out and hiding them.

When Reno found out that the doctors had ordered him to stay overnight for observation, he'd brightened up. He immediately started cajoling the staff to bring him food. After that, he whined and begged for more. He attempted to bribe and extort. He even tried demanding food.

The ER was unusually short of patients that night. The only other patient was an unconscious and very elderly man who had suffered a heart attack after having been struck by a car. Reno's left hand was cuffed to the rail on his hospital bed. There was a uniformed officer, Jennings, the same officer who accompanied him from the D Street station, assigned to guard him. Jennings spent most of his time chatting with the nurse at the central desk. Reno didn't need close watching. Where was he gonna run to, even if he could run? Where was he gonna hide?

But Reno had a plan. He pressed his call button, and a light went on at the central desk.

"Oh no. Mr. Reno again." The young nurse who was chatting with the cop said.

"He probably wants more food. Let him wait, Carol. The fat bastard!" Jennings said.

"Officer Jennings!" the nurse said with mock scorn. "Let's have a little compassion for our calorically challenged citizens."

Jennings watched her walk down the hall to Reno's room. Nurse Carol knew he was watching. She walked that special walk, and she could shake it. She looked back at him as he raised his sight back up to eye level.

"What is it, Mr. Reno?" she asked as she entered his room.

"I think I can finally go to the bathroom now, dear," Reno said with an angelic smile, proud of himself.

The nurse got a bedpan out from under the bed, but Reno protested.

"No, please, dear. I can walk to the bathroom across the hall there. Please, I can't use that!"

"Let me see," Carol said, and walked back up to where Jennings was looking over the sports page.

"Jennings, I want him to use the bathroom across the hall."

"I don't know about that, Carol. He's a dangerous criminal."

"Then you go stick the bedpan under his butt and dump it out when he's finished!"

"Let's go, I'll take the cuffs off and he can walk across the hall," Jennings said, giving up quickly as they walked down the hall to Reno's room. Jennings took his cuff key out of his back pocket, stuck it into the handcuff keyhole, and freed the Trashman's hand. Reno watched closely as Jennings put the key back into his back left pocket.

"You're not going to act up, are you Reno?" Jennings asked.

"No sir. I'll just make this as quick and easy as possible."

"You take as long as it takes, Reno," Jennings instructed.

Reno tiptoed on his little bird feet, maneuvered his huge frame through the doorway and into the relatively small bathroom.

The nurse and the cop walked down the hall a bit and began their flirtatious banter again. They were discussing the therapeutic benefits of uninhibited casual sex when Reno finally emerged. The nurse returned to the central desk as Reno obediently shuffled his way across the hall and onto his bed.

"You really don't even have to handcuff me, officer, I'll be a good boy." Reno sheepishly said as Jennings followed him into his room and put one cuff around the bed rail.

"S.O.P., Reno. It means standard operating procee..." Jennings began, but Reno's right hand had shot up and grabbed him by the throat. Reno had long fingers and strong hands.

He pulled Jennings head down near his face.

"I know what S.O.P. means, blue boy!"

The Big Man was extremely strong, and it took all of Jennings strength and both hands to bring Reno's left hand down to the open handcuff. When Reno's hand was close enough, Jennings snapped the cuff around Reno's wrist.

"Think you got me, cop? Think you got me?" Reno hissed. He pulled Jennings head down to the rail. He had one hand around Jennings' throat, the other on his chin.

"If you go anywhere, you'll be taking this bed with you, fat bastard!" Jennings strained to say as Reno choked him. The cop fumbled for his gun.

"Wrong!" He whispered into Jennings' ear. Then Reno twisted his head sharply and snapped the neck of Officer Jennings. He reached inside the cop's back pocket and pulled out the handcuff key. Reno was getting out of the cuffs as Nurse Carol pushed the curtain open, and Jennings' lifeless body slumped to the floor.

"What happened?" she screamed.

"We were talking. I think he's sick!" Reno said.

As the nurse bent over Jennings, Reno bent over her and then pulled her up by the hair. He admired her pretty neck as he placed one hand on her throat and one hand over her mouth and chin. Her wide eyes looked at him in horror. Before she could try to scream, Reno moved one hand to the top of her head and his other hand to her chin. He twisted her head sharply around, and a crunching snap echoed through the ER as Nurse Carol's neck broke.

Reno put both bodies in his bed, covering them up with the sheet and blanket. He drew the curtain around the bed, then stopped for a moment to admire his work, as if he thought Carol and Jennings made a lovely couple.

Reno waddled down to the central desk. He picked up the register of patients currently under intensive care, and scanned the list. After dropping the register onto the floor, he made his way out into the hall and headed for the private room section on the eighth floor.

CHAPTER 38

Under the Stars

It was a little strange waking up as the sun went down. It reminded me of my rookie years. A lot of water has passed under the bridge since then. For the first year and a half after I'd joined the Boston Police force, I worked from midnight to 8 a.m. I would wake up at about 7:30 p.m. and eat supper, then I would do a few errands or chores, take a shower, and start to get ready for work on the midnight shift. In the morning when I got home, I'd have breakfast, usually a bowl of cereal and a couple of beers. I'd try to go to sleep, but the birds would be chirping, people would be up and moving about, cars starting up as the traffic got heavier, the sun rising in the sky. My life was upside down. It was weird.

I felt pretty good just waking up this evening. I was glad I'd gotten some sleep. I didn't remember dreaming at all. I was stiff and sore, but I felt stronger. I felt like I was going to get better and better. Things got better after awhile, didn't they? Time wounds all heels.

I wondered if my brother, my attorney, would make it up to the hospital that night for my interview with the detectives. I picked at some more hospital food and wondered if and when I would be getting out of there. I wondered where I might be going when I did. Reno had told the investigators I'd thrown Joe Panetta out of his third-floor window, and I guessed he'd also told them I'd tried to kill him.

The young doctor and the scornful nurse came into my room. The nurse handed me the usual array of pills. A dinner tray of spaghetti and salad was put on my bedside table. I suggested a red Bordeaux with tonight's entree' and got the scowl of the nurse instead. The Teen Doc and the nurse changed the bandages on my chest and gave me a sling to help keep my shoulder immobile.

"Nurse, do you know if my brother has been by to see me? Or my, uh, fiancée'?"

"The detectives from the state police and Boston police just left my office," the doctor replied. "I advised them that you had the tube removed today, and they agreed to talk to you tomorrow morning. I told them you needed more rest. More rest and less stress."

"Don't we all, Doc? I mean, what I really need is a vacation. Do you think you could prescribe that? Maybe a week or two, in Florida? Play a little golf. If I were a little older, maybe I'd move to Florida, where the silver- haired folk dwell. Florida is God's waiting room, you know. I could take you with me, Doc."

"Sounds good. Anyway, the cops left orders with the officer outside, you weren't to have any other visitors."

"Your real fiancée', the pretty girl with the long brown hair and pretty green eyes, was here with your brother. The detectives talked to them before they left, and I heard them say they were coming back early tomorrow morning," the nurse told me before she and the young doctor left.

I had an information pipeline set up in the hospital. I was developing sources. You couldn't keep a good detective down. Things were falling back into place.

I got up slowly and walked to the window. Every step I took shook my chest and caused pain, but it felt good to be up. I sat down on the warm radiator by the window looking out from the eighth floor over the city. I was grateful to be alive and still in the game.

Everything seemed to be in order. The city was lit up like a treasure chest of glorious jewels shining in the night. The night sky a twinkling backdrop of multicolored gems. Under the stars, airplanes crossed the sky toward their destinations, their red and green lights blinking in the night. Along Storrow Drive, the white headlights of inbound traffic formed a moving string of pearls, the red taillights of the outbound, a matching set of precious rubies. Below, tiny people walked along sidewalks, and in and out of stores and buildings. Cars proceeded down the streets below in an orderly fashion, stopping for red lights, and moving on the green. Things seemed to be falling into place. Maybe order was about to be restored in my life.

CHAPTER 39

The Monster Lives

I was still staring out the window into the Boston night when I heard the commotion outside my hospital room door—a muffled voice, a thud, and a loud crack, then a sound like a body slumping to the floor just outside my door.

I left my window perch, walked slowly and painfully to the door, and opened it. The uniformed officer was standing there staring at me with the strangest look on his face.

"Is everything all right? I wasn't going anywhere. I heard all the noise, and...you look like you've seen a ghost," I said.

He fell straight forward towards me. As I stepped aside, his face hit the bedside table, knocking my tray of half-eaten spaghetti and salad onto the floor. The dead officer hit the floor with a thud. Then I saw the largest human being I had ever seen in my life, standing before me. He stepped forward and filled the doorway. A guttural, gurgling chuckle came from deep within his throat. He looked at me with delight, his eyes flashing as they peered out from the rolls of flab that made up his face. He chuckled louder and louder, until he roared insanely with laughter. He stepped inside my room, pushing the officer's body aside with his foot, and shut the door.

His mood began to change from insane merriment to just plain insane. He was mad and getting madder.

"What's this all about, Reno?"

"You!" he said in his throaty, guttural, rasp. "You! You son of a bitch! You think the world revolves around you? Don't you think you're the star of the show? You! Isn't it all about you? Don't you think you can stick your nose into everybody's business?"

A little white spit was visible in the corners of his mouth, which increased my paranoia of being jammed in a small room with a nearly seven hundred pound madman, foaming at the mouth.

He carefully picked up the police officer and put him in my bed, neatly arranging the pillow and blanket over his body. He was almost lovingly brushing back the hair of the deceased, talking to the dead policeman as well as to me, mumbling and spitting his diatribe of venom into the dead policeman's face.

"What's it all about, Reno?" I repeated, a bit more loudly, hoping that maybe someone would hear.

"You're what it's all about Jack!" Reno growled. "With your snooping. And prying. What did Bella tell you about the book? Are you going to blackmail me, too? I've chased that book through a dozen people, and they're all dead now. All but you." The Big Man confessed.

The Human Blob was moving toward me, his fat hands moving out from his enormous body, cutting me off from the door. Like a rampaging elephant run amuck. He was possessed, and I was the focus of his rage.

"You, Jack!" he growled.

I was wondering if this guy could crush me with the weight of his huge frame. And I was wondering where the hospital security was.

"You're trapped like a rat, Jack!" Reno said with delight.

I made a desperate leap, trying to go over Reno, like a halfback trying to get over the top of the front line in a goal line defense. I was up, and flying over, just about to break the plane of the goal line when Reno caught me in mid air and pulled me down by the waist. I hit the floor, getting the wind knocked out of me, and the pain in my chest deepened. Then he fell on me.

I couldn't breathe. My bones felt like they were going to break. The gunshot wound was opening up, stitches were popping, and I felt a hot pain traveling up and down the wound channel. My question was answered—this guy could crush me if he fell on me.

Jumbo whispered into my ear with his hot, stinking breath.

"All those bodies. All those soft necks! And I still couldn't catch up to the book! I was always one step behind. First my accountant tried to blackmail me with it, and tried to give it to the state investigator. Then the book went to the nightclub manager and the captain of the Northsea where he stayed. But that transvestite stole it from the Northsea and gave it to the Channel's computer guy just before I got to the cross-dressing freak. Oh, but I got to him all right!

I left him hanging from a light pole at the airport with his pretty blue chiffon dress blowing in the breeze!" The Fat Man shook with laughter. Then he began to shout.

"And the others that got in the way. We finally thought we had it back after I snapped that special investigator's neck on Pier 4. Then my own Bella took it before I could destroy it, and you stole it from her car," his voice quaked. "She wanted to hurt me! They all wanted to hurt me. You want to hurt me! That book can destroy us!"

"Who's us?" I managed to ask, struggling to get some air, my shoulder aching.

"I will not go down alone. Now the cops have it don't they? But they don't know what it is. And you're not going to live to tell them about it. You're the last one! Then we'll clean up the mess."

"Who's we?" I hissed as I began to lose consciousness from lack of air and passed out.

Like a nightmare I couldn't escape from, I slowly regained consciousness. Reno had slid off of me as we lay on the floor by the bed, and was idly brushing back my hair, as he had done with the dead cop. He had a sick smile on his bulbous face. I was drifting back into reality. I knew I had to end this.

He began whispering in my ear again. This guy was right out of his mind, not wrapped too tight. Jelly Belly's antenna wasn't picking up all the channels. His receiver was off the hook. He was a few clowns short of a circus.

He whispered to me. "I used to go out back at the dump my grandfather owned. And I would find the rats. I would find them and I would kill them. I would set out traps with the rotting, stinking garbage they loved the best. I hunted them every chance I got. At first I would hit them with a shovel, a stick, or a rock. And sometimes that would just knock them out. I loved to knock them out. Out cold!" He was chuckling and snorting, his belly shaking.

I was wondering where the hell the hospital staff and the cops were. "Yeah, I know, a depraved childhood. I'm sure it was rough," I said sarcastically.

"What would you know about it, pretty boy?" Reno screamed in his hoarse garble into my ear. I couldn't believe he had resorted to name calling.

The Fat Man held me in his vise-like grip. He was stronger than I thought he might be. He held me like a rag doll. He pulled me on his lap and began to rock back and forth. His hot stinking breath filled my ear and crossed my face as he whispered in gargled tones.

"Out cold. Knocked out cold! Then came the best part. I would pick them up in my hands and watch them slowly wake up again. The big, big rats, and the little rats. I know how they think. I'd put my little fingers around their throats and on top of their heads, and just as they would wake and look up at me with their beady little eyes, I would twist their heads and hear that little snap!" He shook with delight.

I struggled with his hands as he searched for a position around my throat. I was on my back, and I knew if he covered me again with his wall of flab, I might not survive. My wounded shoulder was numb with pain, but this was no time to hold back. This was it. My mind raced. This was no place to die.

My eyes darted around on the floor, looking for anything that could be used as a weapon. I could not get free to reach for the dead policeman's gun. Only a plate of cold, half-eaten spaghetti and some salad lay within my grasp. Maybe I should offer it to him. A little

bite to eat. I wondered how hungry he was. That was probably why

he was so cranky. He hadn't eaten. Maybe if I suggested we go out

for dinner, he'd forget the whole thing.

"Vengeance is mine!" he groaned from the depths of his sewer

pipe throat. I guess dinner was out.

He was maneuvering his blanket of fat on top of me again and I

knew I may not get back up. I was getting desperate. His hands

pushed for my throat and face as he continued.

"I will have my vengeance! Sweet retribution. You're the last

one who knows about the book. I'm going to snap your little neck.

Revenge!"

"Revenge is a dish best served cold!" I growled back at him

quoting Shakespeare as best I could. I scooped up the cold spaghetti

and slapped it into his face, twisting and rubbing it in.

He released my throat and instinctively wiped the cold pasta from

his eyes. He looked at me, wide eyed. He couldn't believe it. I

thought maybe I was onto something, so I picked up the salad and

threw it into his face. He leaned back and howled, probably more from the insult than the oil and vinegar salad dressing in his eyes. He wiped off the salad and glared at me. And as he lunged back at me, I hit him square in the face with the heavy dinner plate, breaking it into pieces.

He was momentarily dazed, blood streaming from his nose and upper lip. Then he came at me again. I plunged the jagged piece of plate remaining in my hand into his left eye socket and gave it a twist. Now he was howling with more than indignation.

The Trash Man reeled back in pain, and I slid my legs out from underneath him. I got to my feet as he pulled the jagged weapon from his eye. I was hoping Reno would beg me to alert medical assistance as the blood squirted out from between the fingers of his hand as it covered his eye.

But now he was really mad.

He dove forward, reaching for my legs. I jumped back, avoiding his grasp, and headed for the door. Reno moved forward from his crouched position like a linebacker just as I got the door half-open. He hit the door as I put my shoulder between it and the doorframe and it closed directly on the wound. The stabbing pain was excruciating, and I felt as if my shoulder were coming apart, as I pushed my body

through the doorway and out into the hall.

CHAPTER 40

Dead End

I had taken a few steps down the hallway towards a light when Reno came through the door behind me. I didn't really know where I was. I had been brought into the hospital unconscious, and hadn't done any exploring yet other than a ride to x-ray. The corridor took a sharp right turn, and then there was another corridor even more desolate.

"Hey! Where is everybody? Security! Police! Hey, who's minding the store?" I yelled.

Reno took the corner and was about ten feet behind me. He was huffing and puffing, sweating and grunting. Blood ran down from his left eye over the rolls of fat and down his face. His huge frame made the corridor seem small as I glanced back at him. I don't think either of us could break into a full run. Blood seeped out of my chest and trickled down my back.

"How about some help here! Medic!" I shouted.

The corridor ahead was a dead end but there was a glowing red emergency exit sign and what appeared to be a door. I picked up the pace as best I could, and hit the emergency bar across the door. A buzzer sounded as I stepped out into the night air and onto an old fire escape eight floors above an alley.

I slammed the door behind me and braced myself against it. Reno hit the door with his tremendous weight, knocking me back and almost over the metal railing of the fire escape.

I held the door and got back into position, but I was losing the battle. I looked downward for help, but the only sign of life was a garbage truck unloading a Dumpster below—probably one of Reno's, anyway.

Just as I realized my task was insurmountable, I suddenly released the door. Reno fell out onto the fire escape with a crash. The bolts holding the old metal frame to the brick building began to pop, and the fire escape plunged two feet out and then about four feet down.

As the fire escape swayed to a creaking halt, Reno and I realized that we held each other. Neither of us wanted to move too quickly.

"Why don't we settle this like men? A game of chess perhaps? A staring contest? How about a one-mile foot race two weeks from Sunday?" I pleaded.

He moved to grab me by the throat. I shifted and threw a kick to his groin, hoping I could find it. More bolts holding the old fire escape to the hospital wall popped, and we dropped another four feet. Reno lost his balance as the deck tipped, and got partly tossed over the side of the fire escape. He was able to get his hands around a couple of the rusty metal rails. He was hanging over the side. Another bolt popped, and we dropped another foot.

Now Reno was even further over the side of the fire escape, holding on to the top rail with both of his strong hands. His feet were kicking in the air, but he could not manage to pull his enormous weight back onto the platform.

"Help me!" he commanded.

"Help you! You're one of those people that just takes up space in this world, Reno. And in your case, you take up a lot of space. You don't contribute, you consume! You turn everything into garbage, don't you?" I yelled back, feeling like an angry god with the power of life or death.

"Help me!" Reno hissed as I looked down at the garbage truck lifting and emptying the Dumpster below. The fire escape swayed and creaked.

"Like you helped the accountant, Joe Panetta, Reno? Your punks threw him out a window, shot him, and then you ran over him with a car. Twice! Like you helped Bella, Reno? You beat her, snapped her neck, and left her in that rail car. Like the midget? The accountant whose neck you broke before you threw him off the Mystic Tobin Bridge? The transvestite you killed and left hanging from the runway lights at Logan, Reno? Like you helped all the others, you sick bastard? Is that the kind of help you want, Fatboy?" There, I'd said it. I'd called him Fatboy, to his fat face...and it felt good. I couldn't be a sensitive guy all the time.

"Help me! You've got to help me! You're a cop."

"I don't know, Reno, I've got this bad shoulder, you know? Where you shot me…"

"Help me, I can't hold on much longer!"

"You said the book could destroy 'Us,' Reno. Who else is involved? Who else would go down with you?"

"Just pull me in! I'm slipping!" he demanded.

The bolts were creaking and straining. I was wondering how I could let go of my grip on the rail and try to pull in six hundred and fifty pounds of fat that wanted to kill me. Then the twisted metal shrieked, bolts popped, and the fire escape dropped several feet again.

"Talk Fatman, or we're going to see if you bounce!"

Reno glanced downward, his body shook, and I could see the terror in his eyes.

"I'm in business with Lieutenant Governor Paul King! He started funneling me the big state contracts, and I kicked back tons of money his way. It was his idea! He came to me years ago. He's obsessed to be the next governor. He knows the present governor is going to run for the Senate. He wants to be governor so bad, he can taste it! The book shows the skim off the top, the tax fraud, and lists the other businesses involved. They're all friends of King's! Now help! I can't...hold..."

I was thinking that this was a great way to interrogate someone— ask questions when they're hanging from a fire escape eight floors up. Reno was suddenly very talkative.

I moved along the rail, closer to him. "Reno. That book can't tie Lieutenant Governor King in with your business. You'll go down alone!"

"King made a fortune from me and my business! And I contributed even more, to secret funds. I've got times, dates, and places, all written down. I got pictures of him and me. I got canceled checks. I've got receipts for trips and gifts. I've got it all. And I'll give it to you! Just let me up! I'm slipping!"

So that's what this is all about. Reno and King would be front-page news. Major scandal. "LT. GUV & SERIAL KILLER IN BED TOGETHER," "RACE FOR GUV TURNS TO TRASH," or "SERIAL KILLER CLAIMS LT. GOV. AS LAST VICTIM."

Reno had snapped the necks of a dozen people, and he was still trying to save his business. I guessed he'd say anything at this point.

I moved very slowly over to the outside of the fire escape, looking for the safest way to grab him and attempt to pull him in. As the fire escape creaked and swayed slightly, I could see Reno had stopped trying to pull his big legs up. He was running out of energy. His fat, sweaty fingers were losing their grip as he switched from hand to hand, trying to reaffirm his grasp. I could see him glancing to the street below with horror.

As I was trying to grab a big arm or a big, fat leg, I heard voices from above. There were two Boston cops and an orderly standing in the emergency doorway, looking down at us.

"Call for a ladder truck! And throw me your belt and a pair of handcuffs!" I shouted over the racket the garbage truck below was making.

Reno was wheezing, and his fingers were getting bloody from the old, rusty, cast iron fire escape. I ripped off the top of my hospital pajamas and tied Reno's wrist to the metal frame. I looked up to see a cop pulling a pair of handcuffs off his belt, but Reno couldn't hold on any longer. As I looked down, he looked up at me with an insane grin.

"I'll see you in hell, Jack!"

As his fingers slipped from the fire escape and the pajama top ripped away, he added, "Don't be late!"

As he slipped away, he stared into my face, his intense eyes glaring out from the rolls of fat. He seemed to move away slowly as he hurtled downward, screaming all the way down, his huge frame turning slowly in the air. A two-and-a-half gainer. I gave it a nine.

I cringed as Reno landed squarely in the back of the garbage truck, with a crunching thud, on top of a pile of garbage. For a few moments, I stared at his body. I couldn't believe it. I took a deep breath and exhaled slowly as I looked down. The huge threat that was attempting to frame me for a number of murders—the man, who wanted to outright kill me, had just dropped like a sack of rocks, away from me and out of my life. I was stunned.

I even felt a little guilt, about all the names I had called him. I couldn't believe I'd been reduced to such blatant usage of derogatory adjectives. I was a little ashamed. I was usually such a sensitive guy.

Then I saw him moving. Slowly. First his legs a little, then his arms and head. He looked like a small, struggling bug in the truck far below. The cops in the doorway above me were frantically calling on their portables for patrol cars on the street to converge on the alleyway.

The operator of the truck must've hit a button in the cab, because the space Reno was in began to get smaller as the truck's engine got louder. The garbage in the back of the truck was being compressed. And Reno along with it.

As Reno became more and more conscious, he must have realized the world was closing in on him and he was going to be crushed. He struggled to move his mountain of flesh. His bones were broken from his fall. He was groping for anything to hold onto. He was crawling through trash and medical waste toward the front of the garbage truck, looking back at the moving steel wall. The mounds of garbage began to tangle his feet. I couldn't believe he was moving at all after a fall of almost eight floors. But Thaddeus Reno wasn't going anywhere.

He could not outrun the slow moving steel wall. His feet were getting tangled...then his ankles and legs. His screams turned to a muffled gurgling as the garbage surrounded him, pinning him between the converging walls of waste. The trash got tighter and tighter around his legs and waist, as the walls of garbage began to encompass him, almost straightening him up onto his feet. The walls were beginning to crush him. His final gargled screams were muffled as his circumference was encircled by garbage and compressed.

Over the roar of the garbage truck's engine, I thought I heard some of his bones snap as Reno was engulfed and condensed into a block of garbage. Only one bloody hand had emerged, reaching upward.

CHAPTER 41

The Man Who Would Be King

Summer had turned into late fall, but today it was still above seventy degrees in Boston. It was the glorious end to Indian Summer. The sunshine was flooding through my hospital room windows. It was another clean and glorious morning, another chance, and a golden opportunity. Sometimes you just have to stop and go for what you really want.

I was still asleep and dreaming about Johnny's Jazz and Blues Club when the young doctor came in and began giving me the once-over. I sat up and wiped the sleep from my eyes. He took my blood pressure, temperature, looked in my ears, and at my tongue. Then he gave me two injections, one for infection and one for pain.

"You know, Doc, every time you stick a needle in me, somewhere there's a voodoo doll screaming."

As he was leaving he told me there were detectives outside my door, waiting to talk to me.

"Oh, please send them in. I don't want to live another day under their protection. I don't think I could take it."

Jim Watson, Sergeant Bill Rogers, Detective Sergeant Houston, and a young man with wire-rimmed glasses, frizzy, long brown hair, and a long, handlebar mustache all entered my room smiling. They gathered around my bed, and Bill Rogers introduced the young man with the mustache as Assistant District Attorney Jay Thomas. They were still smiling. I smiled back, not knowing why.

"What?" I said, looking from face to face. "What?"

"The newspapers, radio, and television are putting on quite a positive spin for you, Jack!" Bill Rogers said.

Jim Watson added, "They're saying you got the serial killer, Jack. The headlines are reading 'DETECTIVE CAPTURES KILLER,' 'RENO'S ROOFTOP RUMBLE,' 'KRAZY KILLER KRUSHED,' and all that. They're making you out to be a hero."

Detective Sergeant Houston of the state police cleared his throat and got real serious. "Thaddeus Reno has not been officially charged with the serial killings, at this time. The investigation is ongoing. We expect eminent arrests." He looked down at me.

This stuffed shirt was all I could take. He sounded like he was running for office. I'd been through a lot and I guess I boiled over.

"Look! If there's something you want to charge me with, well go ahead and do it! I've been pistol-whipped and chased. Fat Boy tried to run me over with a car, he shot me, he tried to suffocate me and throw me off an eighth floor fire escape. You should be providing me with adequate counsel. And on top of that, I've been eating hospital food for four days! So go ahead and charge me with something, or shove off and see my lawyer!"

"Take it easy, Jack! Reno is dead. They had to pry his bloody body from a block of compressed garbage. And we came here to thank you for your help...and to fill in a few holes, pardon the expression, and get the rest of the story. Your brother and girlfriend are right outside," Jim Watson said, putting his hand on my shoulder.

"Oh...sorry, Jim...Houston, uh...maybe I've got that post-trauma violence syndrome I read about in Newsweek."

"I don't anticipate you being charged with anything, Jack. But we want you to testify," Assistant District Attorney Jay Thomas said.

"You want me to testify? I need to know the answers to some questions. Like do you have any idea what the hell is going on?" I said.

Bill Rogers glanced over at Houston, then sat down on the end of my bed. He began to lay it all out for me as the other guys found more comfortable spots in the room to settle into.

"We had Reno as a suspect since early on, Jack. One of the first victims of the serial killer was Reno's accountant, Paul Moreau."

"He was blackmailing Reno with the book," I added.

"His apartment was broken into and ransacked," Rogers continued. "His computer and every disk he had were stolen. The place was turned upside down. Somebody was looking for something. We made more connections when you told us about the visit you got in your office from Reno, Bella Pavoni, and the midget. After the girl and the midget showed up dead, Reno became our prime suspect. Only in the last few days did we put it together that the computer hack, Gerard Spring, did computer work with Reno's accountant, and they all socialized at The Channel, where the manager got killed and Digby Riggs worked."

"We never really considered you as a suspect. You were only wanted for questioning. We believed you had the answers to some questions, parts of the puzzle, whether you knew it or not," Houston said. He was almost believable.

I was beginning to relax.

"There was guys lookin' out for you, Jack," Jim Watson said, in his charming, colloquial way.

Houston got my attention when he told me Rick O'Hare, the manager at the Channel who was found dead in the parking lot with a broken neck, was an undercover state police detective that had been placed there with the recommendation of a local mobster who owed a favor to someone in the vice squad. Houston said that in O'Hare's darkroom, his partner found surveillance photos of the Lieutenant Governor meeting with Reno on different occasions at The Channel.

"Got some great shots of the Lieutenant Governor in the back lounge with one of them transformers," Jim Watson said.

"Transvestites," I reminded him, being a politically correct, sensitive guy.

"Transistors, transformers—whatever."

Watson continued the story. He told me none of what I had told them had made any sense; there was no motive, until I was shot in the chest by Reno while holding the book in my hand. One of the Boston cops that was up in the Bean Counter's apartment after he was killed had seen similar numbers and columns of numbers on a scratch pad on Joe's work table. When the state police investigators got the book, it didn't take them long to figure out some of the basics, using your friend Joe's scratch pad and notes.

"Panetta had rough estimates of Reno and his partner skimming millions of tax free dollars off the top of his waste management business," Watson continued. "He had figured out the phone numbers of the businesses listed in the back of the book and had even called a couple, listing them on his scratch pad. There were state agencies as well as private companies listed. There were phantom pick-ups and disposals. There were `ghost routes.' But real bills."

"Gentlemen," I interrupted, "I must tell you that although your reasoning is sound, I must remind you that your quarry, Mr. Thaddeus Reno, The Human Blimp, The Round Mound of Pounds, is deceased, and won't be appearing for any trial. What's this about testifying?"

The four looked back and forth at each other, and then the three cops looked at Jay Thomas, the ADA, who looked at me and began scratching his head.

"Well," he began, "we're gathering evidence now to indict Reno's silent partner—"

"You're going after the Lieutenant Governor? You can't be serious. You've got bits and pieces," I said in disbelief. I couldn't believe the boldness of the action.

"One of those bits and pieces is the Lieutenant Governor's large share of stock in Reno Waste Management," Thomas continued. "We picked up three thugs that worked for Reno, two of which were at the murder scene of Joe Panetta. They're pretty scared now that their boss is dead. They're talking a blue streak."

"Bob and Skinny." I said.

"Their real names are Ray, Rick, and Billy Provost. Step-brothers from East Boston," Sergeant Rogers said.

"Some cheap hoods who used to stick up liquor stores and gas stations. Real dirtbags," said Watson.

"You mean misunderstood malcontents, recidivist offenders, or career criminals, don't you?" I politically corrected Watson, being sensitive to unfair labeling.

"What? Career criminals? You make them sound like they got jobs, for Christ's sake!" Watson protested.

"We are executing search warrants at Reno's home, boat, and businesses as we speak," Thomas continued. "We believe with your testimony, the book, as you call it, the undercover officers' reports, Reno's and Lieutenant Governor King's bank records, including his election campaign fund records and statements from the stepbrothers—with all this and a little more, I'm confident that we can show, by a totality of the evidence, that King is guilty of at least tax evasion, and maybe conspiracy to commit some other major felonies."

"He's going down, Jack," Watson stated.

I jumped on the bandwagon. "You may get lucky with those search warrants. Reno told me he had the times, dates, and locations of meetings with King, canceled checks, and receipts for 'gifts.' He said he had some revealing photos of the Lieutenant Governor. And if you can show that King knew the state's special investigator, Henri Riley, had the book just before his neck was snapped on Pier 4…King was supposed to get the book back for Reno."

Sergeant Bill Rogers got his notebook out and was writing. I guess they hadn't heard that one.

Well, that's my story, and I'm stickin' to it. After all…I'm a detective.

—EPILOGUE—

Eight months later, as the April sunshine streamed through the canyons of downtown Boston, I was walking down the federal courthouse steps with my girlfriend, who now really was my fiancée. The trial had finally concluded. Lieutenant Governor Paul King had just been convicted on federal charges of tax evasion and conspiracy to obstruct justice. Reno had left behind many incriminating documents, even more incriminating than the book, more than enough to aid the prosecution in getting the conviction. Former Lieutenant Governor Paul King wouldn't get any hard time, but he would probably get a stretch at one of the cushy Club Fed locations. He wouldn't be running for Governor.

As we walked down the court house steps, that bright Boston afternoon, I heard two young, uniformed cops talking about me.

"Jack's the one that brought down the serial killer, The Snapper, and the Lieutenant Governor," one said.

The other cop smiled. "Yeah, but I heard he got knocked out by a midget."

The end

ABOUT THE AUTHOR

Born in New Bedford, Mass. Johnny attended boarding school in the Berkshires and played harmonica in a weekend blues band in New York City's Greenwich Village in the late '60's. After 2 years at U-Mass Dartmouth, Johnny moved to Boston where he drove a taxicab, attended Berklee School of Music and Harvard University Extension School majoring in Zen Buddhism.

Johnny Barnes sang and played guitar in all of the famous nightclubs in Boston with many of rock and roll's legends, producing and releasing a dozen records. Local airplay and intense record company interest led to a hit song in England and work with legendary producer, Jimmy Miller (The Rolling Stones, Blind Faith with Eric Clapton, Traffic with Steve Winwood.) Barnes moonlighted, helping manage Boston's largest live music nightclub,

The Channel, where his band opened for numerous major acts through the '80's and early 1990's. Barnes was a paralegal investigator for law firms, and an operative and operations manager for Boston area private detective agencies. Johnny worked for Massachusetts's Legal Services, the Mass. ACLU, and was a subcontract homicide investigator for the state's Committee for Public Counsel. Since 1991 Barnes has been a full time Police Officer, a FBI trained Hostage Negotiator, and a Detective.

Printed in the United States
202546BV00001B/82-162/A

9 781410 707932